INKED

SEXY TALES OF TATTOO EROTICA

EDITED BY
ANNA SKY

www.sincyrpublishing.com
sincyr.submissions@gmail.com

Layout by Sexy Little Pages

Print ISBN: 978-1-948780-27-8

CONTENTS

COMPANY INK
BY LILYA LORING

WADE HAD BEEN SWEEPING, wiping down display cases, and running equipment through the autoclave all day. Since he'd passed his bloodborne pathogens course, he'd been allowed to clean all the tattoo artists' bays. It included wiping everything down with a chemical germicide before setting everything up again. He restocked ink cups, replaced bottles of ink in neat rows, and placed new baggies on all the spray bottles. This was between taking phone calls, which were mostly people asking for a price quote. He'd tell them the shop minimum was fifty dollars, and what that'd buy them depended on the artist.

The decor was depressing. A couple of leather sofas that Bob, the owner, brought from his own home, dominated the lobby along with a giant fish tank. The reception counter was a ramshackle affair made of kitchen cabinet remnants. The carpet was thin and had a slight odor to it. The magic he felt for the place when he first started his apprenticeship was gone. This wasn't the glamour he'd imagined when he came into Company Ink clutching his portfolio full of drawings. He didn't have a particular style. Instead, he'd worked countless hours on drawings that would show his range—new school, old school, typical flash, portraits, and even some H.R. Giger inspired oddities. He figured he'd find his niche once he started tattooing.

It took Wade two years to save up the money for a proper apprenticeship. Company Ink didn't look like much, but the artists were amazing, and the shop was in the heart of Five Points in downtown Columbia. Because of its proximity to the university, there was always a fresh supply of students vying for their first tattoos. At the same time, this also meant an influx of drunken sorority girls and frat brothers wanting to get inked.

In general, Wade was a quiet, studious person. Whenever he drew, he became lost in his own little world. He was tall and lanky, a fact exaggerated by the straight leg, dark jeans he always wore. He was unconventionally attractive—wide face, equine nose, and amber colored hair which he wore in a modern quiff with the sides shaved down. With the band shirts, thermal undershirts, hair and Chucks, he had the style down; however, with a body free of any modifications, he didn't look the part of a budding tattoo artist. He also didn't have the ego. Still, Bob gave him a chance; beside cleanup duties, he drew designs and created stencils which were then scrutinized by the other artists. If the designs were good enough, they'd go on the flash wall, and he'd be one step closer to tattooing.

He was still sweeping, lost in thought, and didn't hear Grace approach. "You done in here," she asked in her thick voice.

He blinked a few times before looking at her. She

was wearing her usual "uniform": super tight jeans with lots of holes and a spaghetti strap tank top. Today's shirt hugged her breasts especially well. Her body was thicker, her ass full and round, and her breasts small but pert. With long, blue-black hair with the sides shaved, heavy smoky eyes, a full sleeve of tattoos, and a nose piercing, she was the quintessential tattoo artist.

Wade had a crush on her from the moment he first saw her brooding over a copy of *Leaves of Grass*. She was a total bitch to him, but he found the mystery and contradiction of her irresistible. He'd fantasized about her many times, about bending her over the red, faux leather chair and sliding into her tight pussy.

"Yo, Milk," she snapped and plopped down on her stool. "Finish up and get the hell out of my space."

"Yes, Grace," he said as he remembered the broom in his hand, and resumed sweeping. He hated her nickname for him but tried not to let it show.

Each space was unique to the artist. Rod's was full of skulls of all kinds—mostly the cheap resin deals found at flea markets. Dave, a wannabe gangster, had photos of rappers with heavy gold chains, posters of women with their asses hanging out, and almost a complete collection of Homies toys lined up in neat rows. Wade liked Grace's bay the best, and it wasn't just because he was hot for her. A geek at heart, the walls and shelves were covered with *Star Wars,* Super Mario, and *Doctor Who* collectibles. She also had a clear obsession with 80s movies given the collection of DVDs she played on a small monitor as she worked. She knew the dialogue of dozens of films by heart.

Whereas the other bays were all for show, this was an expression of Grace and her passions.

He wanted her, badly, but she typically only acknowledged him enough to tell him to do something or provide criticism, which he appreciated, of one of his designs.

With a sigh, he returned to his post at the front counter. He was working on a new design: a locked heart with Isis wings. It wasn't the most original design, but he tried to put his spin on it. He was too busy coloring and shading with his pencils to notice the buxom blond who sauntered in.

She peered over the counter, watching Wade's hands as they moved.

"Beautiful," she said.

He looked up and made eye contact with her. Her eyes were the icy blue you usually only see on TV or in the movies. She looked to be in her mid-twenties, close to Wade in age. Her skin was tan, hair a soft blond—not bleached. The curve of her jaw was sharp and was accentuated by a row of six sparkling earrings running up each ear like constellations. If Grace was winter, this woman was summer.

He stood slowly, hoping not to trip over his own feet. "Thanks," he said.

Her breasts were ample, pouring over the top of a low cut, draped tunic dress. *I bet you could fit a whole pack of smokes in that cleavage*, he thought. Her arms were covered in a forest of flowers, butterflies, birds, and vines that started at her left wrist and splashed onto her collarbone. It was beautiful work.

She smiled widely, "Do you have a book?"

He ran his hand through his hair and grinned. "No, I'm just an apprentice."

"What a pity," she pretended to pout then bit at her highly glossed lower lip. "Well, maybe I can be your first. I like what you are working on back there." She ran her fingertips up and down his bicep. He was instantly hard, his cock straining against the fabric of his jeans. "Promise you'll save it for me?" She licked her lips.

"Uh, ok," he said. His heart was racing.

"Say," she leaned in even closer, "I need to loosen up a bit before my tat. What say we go to the back room?"

"I, uh," he stammered, torn between desire and his sense of decorum. *What if Grace saw?*

She didn't wait for him to finish, just reached over the counter and massaged his cock through his jeans. "Meet me in five," she said, as she turned and walked off.

He watched her ass as she moved, the fabric of her dress rising and falling along the tops of her thighs. This wasn't the first time he'd been propositioned at Company Ink, but he'd never met anyone as forward as... he didn't even know her name.

A couple of minutes later, he poked his head around the doorway. Grace was at her table, headphones on as she worked on a design transfer. She was in the zone and until she finished; he knew she wouldn't notice his absence. The only issue would be if a customer came in.

He walked over to Rod's bay. "I'm going to take a break. That cool?"

Rod looked up from his computer screen and smiled broadly. "The blond huh," he said.

Wade nodded. "You know her?"

"Liv. She's a regular, gets a lot of work done here. Have fun my man." He chuckled and turned his eyes back to the screen.

The back room was just as thrown together as the front. There was an old, worn couch, dining table, and a mock kitchenette consisting of a microwave, mini-fridge, and a hot plate. Sometimes the employees crashed, or engaged in other activities, on the couch. While the door didn't lock, it did provide a bit of necessary privacy. It was far from sexy but after months of pining for Grace, Wade desperately needed the release.

As he walked toward Liv, she pulled at the front of her dress. Her breasts tumbled free of the draped, aqua fabric. They were full and tan like the rest of her. He wanted to take one in his mouth, but she pushed him down roughly on the couch. She kissed him, hard, and his tongue explored her mouth as he fondled her breasts.

Within moments, she had his fly down and his cock in her fingers. He was solid with need and pumped in and out of her hand a few times before she pulled her panties to one side and straddled him. Her cunt was wet and Wade slid in easily. He watched as she threw her head back and gasped whilst he sucked one of her nipples. He'd never done anything like this, and it thrilled him. He wasn't sure how long he would last.

Liv ground into him. She was a live wire, convulsing and contracting around him. Her eyes were closed. He could see the gold sparkle of her eyeshadow as it shimmered in the light. She was the one in control. The best he could do was hold on and make sure she that as she glided up and down his length, he didn't come out of her. The slapping of their bodies and their ragged breaths were the only sounds they made. Her breasts dangled in his face as he guided her with his hands on her ass.

Her thrusting slowed as he again took one of her nipples into his mouth. He sucked, long and hard, trying to take in as much of her as he could. Wrapping his arms around her, he came, his cock still pumping into her. Her body shook and he could feel her orgasm, feel her tighten around him and ride him hard for a few furious moments.

They stayed that way for several seconds, then Liv giggled and stood up. "I feel much more relaxed," she said.

As she adjusted her clothing, the door to the backroom opened. Wade was still on the couch with his cock out, glistening from Liv's juices.

"Oops, looks like mommy's home," Liv half-whispered and gave him a wolfish smile.

"Liv," Grace called from the doorway. She looked Wade up and down, no doubt noting his nakedness. Her arms were crossed and her eyes blazed as she looked down her sharp nose at him. Wade knew that look. She was hella pissed. The look passed, and she smiled at Liv. "You're late, bitch," she said.

Liv chuckled, "Yeah well, I was just talking to..."

"Wade," he said quietly as he tucked himself into his jeans and zipped them up.

"Wade. He's going to do a tat for me when he's ready."

"Isn't that nice," Grace replied. Her voice was all sugar, but her words were tinged with poison.

Wade didn't understand Grace's reaction. She seemed, well, jealous. "But she hates me," he said to himself in the bathroom mirror after cleaning up. He opened the door and returned to his station at the front. From there, he had to crane his neck to watch Grace work on Liv. Grace's head was down and she was already transferring the stencil she'd prepared. The finished work would be a tiger in the style of a brush painting. It started three inches above her knee and reached her hip. The tattoo would definitely take more than one session. Grace had to keep lifting Liv's skirt higher and higher; the sight filled his mind with all sorts of dirty thoughts. *Those two could definitely get into some trouble together.*

It was over two hours before Liv left. On her way out, she winked at Grace and said, "Have at him. I'll see you later, sexy bitch."

Grace didn't even look at Wade. Instead she stomped back to her bay, her leather boots thudding heavily on the tiles. Wade locked the door and stared out of the glass for a long time. She didn't call him to come clean things up, which was unusual.

"Wade," she called just as he was packing up to leave for the night.

Rod had already left and Dave hadn't even come in, so the shop was quiet save for Grace's TV. She was watching *Legend* again. When he approached, she was setting things out on her counter and didn't turn to look at him. Her pale skin glowed softly under her work lamp. He wanted to kiss her shoulder blades, press himself into her as he slid his hand around to cup her breasts.

When she sensed him behind her, she went rigid. "Wade?"

"Yes?"

"What do you think of Liv," she asked.

"Liv," he blinked, unsure how to respond.

"You know, the overly friendly blond," she sighed. "Do you think she's hot?"

His throat felt tight, and he wondered if it was a trick question. Some verbal trap she'd concocted to embarrass him. Though his fingers shook, he reached out to touch a tendril of her silky black hair. It surprised him when she didn't turn on him, didn't shrug him away.

"Well," she said in almost a whisper.

"She's hot, and we had fun," he said. "But she's not..." he paused.

She turned, scanning his face with her dark eyes. "Not what?" she said.

He gulped, his palms were sweaty. "Not you. She's not you."

"I was hoping you'd say that," she smiled.

She closed the gap between them and ran her hands up and down his back, pressing her body against him. He was instantly hard with longing. Slipping his hands under the thin straps of her tank top, he pulled them aside. He kissed her shoulder delicately and gave it a gentle bite.

"Ah, fuck," she said, grinding her crotch against his in response.

Grace guided him back to the red leather chair and he all but fell into it. Walking around him, she let down the latch and the back reclined. He inhaled sharply as she straddled him. He could feel the heat emanating from her pussy. Freeing a breast from her shirt, he kissed around the curve of it before flicking her nipple with his tongue. He was glad she wasn't wearing a bra, as it gave him easy access.

"Shit," she said as she rode him hard. Abruptly, she leaned back, forcing him to release her hard nipple from his mouth.

"There's only one problem," she said.

"What," he panted.

"I don't fuck guys who aren't tatted," she stood quickly.

"Well, I guess it's a good thing you're a tattoo artist."

"I was hoping you'd say that too. Tell me, Wade, can I be your first?" Her face was lit with mischief.

"Yeah," he smiled timidly, "but are you really going to leave me this way?" He pointed at his painfully engorged cock and almost whimpered. Almost.

Grace grinned, walked over to her rolling stool, and slid it over to the chair. "I can do a little something," she said.

She unbuckled his belt and pulled it off in a swift motion. Next came the button and zipper. He tried to help her, but she batted his hands away. "Don't make me tie you down," she laughed.

He watched her hands as she took his cock out of

his boxers. Her hands were warm and sure as she began to stroke him from shaft to tip. "Nice," she said.

Her hair fell as she moved her face toward him. He could only see the blue-black shine of her hair, feeling her breath as her lips moved closer. She licked the tip of his cock slowly, teasingly, then blew on it lightly. The cool rush of air sent waves of pleasure through his body. She giggled at his reaction, enjoying watching him squirm.

As she leaned in again, she sucked him in earnest, taking him fully into her mouth. Wade moaned and flexed his feet, willing himself not to come too quickly. The feel of her mouth was exquisite and, even though he tried to hold back, he began thrusting into her. Her free hand explored his thighs and cupped his balls. The longer she continued, the more eager she was with her movements until he was deep in her throat, his hips rising off the chair, wanting more of her, more of her than was possible.

He gripped the armrests as he climaxed, coming hard in her mouth. She didn't seem to mind, squeezing his shaft to prolong the orgasm. Head thrown back, he panted, bewildered momentarily by the euphoria. He heard her get up and walk toward the bathroom.

"Wait," he called hoarsely. "Don't you want me to return the favor?"

"Nah, Milk," she said with her back to him. "We've got work to do. I left something for you on my table. Check it out."

"Say, think you could stop calling me Milk now?"

She looked over her shoulder, hair bouncing down her shoulder blades, "I don't know. Think you can get a tan?" She winked and walked into the bathroom.

***

It took Wade a while to get the energy to zip up his pants, put his belt back on, and head over to the table. There, amid different designs, was a large image already prepped for transfer. He recognized the elongated, sloping head immediately. It was a Xenomorph, Grace's interpretation of H.R. Giger's concept art for the film *Alien*. The design was circular in nature, with the alien's tail curving in an unnatural arc toward its mouth, almost like an Ouroboros. It was dark, far darker than the creatures in the film had been. She had maintained Giger's style but instead of the gauzy, muted effect of his palette, her lines were crisp and sharp.

He held it in his hands for a long time, envisioning what it would look like on skin. If it were him, he'd place it on the top of the shoulder, spiraling out as an epaulette. Tiptoeing, Grace walked up behind him.

"So?" she asked, quietly.

"It's awesome!" he said. "Shoulder piece?"

"That's what I was thinking," she moved around him so she could study his expression.

"It's gonna be sick. Who's it for?"

She rolled her eyes, "You, dumbass. I designed it for you."

It suddenly clicked that she'd been planning this, that despite her tough demeanor, she was not only attracted to him, but had also gone out of her way to create something he'd love.

"How'd you know," he raised an eyebrow.

"What, that *Alien* is your all-time favorite movie, or that you have an unhealthy obsession with H.R. Giger?" She shrugged, "Don't worry, I'm not cyberstalking you. I just pay attention."

He laughed. "It's perfect."

"So, you want it?" she had that wicked smile again.

***

Grace spent the next two-and-a-half hours outlining the design. It was going to be large, spanning from the middle of his bicep up and across to his collarbone. She was smart about the placement though; Wade could easily show it off with a sleeveless shirt or cover it with a regular t-shirt. He was after all, still an apprentice. Knuckle tattoos were a way off into the future, if he stuck with it.

He admired her beauty as she worked, dark hair falling across her face as she mouthed the dialogue from *Labyrinth*, though it wasn't the same lust he felt earlier. Now, he was watching an artist at work, studying the way she held the tattoo machine, selected needles, and the way she shaped the lines. It was difficult keeping track, as he had to keep his head turned whilst reclining in the chair. She was quick and had a light touch, but it was still painful—a dull ache that occasionally flared into searing pain. She wiped away blood and excess ink with practiced and fluid movements.

They took a break in the middle of the session, giving Grace some time to rest her tingling fingers. He wanted to kiss her, hold her, but he was exhausted and glad for a reprieve from the pain. Finally, in the early hours of morning, she wiped the completed tattoo down with green soap and told him to go look in the mirror. He wasn't very broad-chested or muscular and didn't really like to be shirtless but as he gazed at his reflection, at the new heavy black lines, he was transformed. He felt more masculine, powerful. He felt a pride in his body he had never had before.

Grace watched him, and he could tell from the desirous look in her eyes that she noticed the change too. He'd seen similar changes before with other customers and was glad of the gift she gave to him. He knew her choice wasn't without risk. Bob would give her hell if he found out about her staying late to do a free tattoo. Wade strutted back to her and kissed her roughly on the mouth.

As she spread ointment on the tattoo and wrapped it in cling film, she said, "It's late, but do you want to head back to my place?"

Wade was tired and his shoulder throbbed, but his desire hadn't subsided. His cock stiffened as he imagined actually fucking her, his Grace. "We'd have to be careful," he said, pointing to his shoulder.

She shook her head and laughed, "Don't worry. I won't touch your new tat."

As they walked out to their cars together, he held one hand low on her hip. The energy between them was electric, more than it had been earlier that night. Allowing her to permanently mark his body had created an intimate bond.

***

Wade didn't waste any time once they got to her apartment. As soon as the door closed and she slid the lock home, he pressed her against the wall, his arms tight around her. He kissed her collarbone, working his way up to her mouth. Yes, he'd had crushes before, but he had never wanted a woman as much as he did Grace.

"I want to fuck you right here," he whispered into her ear.

"Slow down, cowboy," she said as she gently pushed him away. "I have a roommate. Pretty sure she's out, but you never know."

She walked ahead of him, reaching one hand back for him to hold, and guided him through the dimly lit apartment. As expected, there was a lot of metal and leather, but what surprised him were the bursts of bright color: aqua, coral, chartreuse, and mint. It was beautiful but in a soft way. He'd half expected some sort of heavy metal dungeon but he was wrong. Fresh white gardenias with sprigs of lavender sat in a vase on the glass coffee table. There were shelves covered with books—mostly poetry—and vintage, black and white photographs on the wall. It was eclectic, yet everything seemed to fit.

He stood, open-mouthed, taking in his surroundings. When Grace felt the resistance of his hand, which stopped her in her tracks, she turned to look at him.

"Surprised?" She raised an eyebrow.

"Well, yeah, a little. I mean, I expected…" his eyes scanned the room as if the right word were lurking there somewhere.

"Something darker? Maybe a coffin and some rubber bats?" She laughed, but it was a good natured laugh. She reached forward, massaging his cock through the thick denim, "I have many sides," she said. "And I always appreciate beauty where I find it."

He let her lead him on into the bedroom. The whole situation felt surreal. If it weren't for the pain in his shoulder, he would have thought he was dreaming. This was Grace, the woman he'd fantasized about for months and now, now he was in his apartment and was going to do all the naughty things he envisioned. How many times he'd touched himself, stroked himself languidly and then with increasing fervor, while he thought about her breasts, the swell of her hips, the music of her laugh, seeing her tattoos, as she spread herself before him.

Her bedroom was just off the main hall. The room was much darker than the living area with most of the decor in black or tones of gray. The bed sat underneath a large, double window covered in bedding patterned with old school tattoo designs. There was an occasional splash of color but, for the most part, the room was monochromatic. It was almost like being in a cocoon. If asked, he wouldn't have been able to put it into words.

Wade was distracted by looking around the room, at all the things she had, obviously, carefully chosen and placed. He jumped as she stood in front of him, breasts jutting, nipples hard. *When had she taken off her shirt?*

He wasn't surprised to find her pale skin covered in tattoos. Similar to her arms, she liked bright colors mingled with thick black lines on her other artwork. Her ribs were covered with vines in which hid birds, flowers, a rabbit, and a couple of skulls. The vines seemed like a highway, and he wanted to run his tongue along them, slip it up into the space between her breasts.

"Well," Grace said, "are you just going to stare?" It was her usual bitchy tone, but he could tell from the fire in her eyes that she didn't intend to sound cruel.

He grabbed her around the waist, pulling him to her, desperate to finally feel her skin against his. With a grunt, he used one hand to peel away his t-shirt, gasping when he caught the freshly bandaged tattoo.

She smiled at him sweetly and helped him free his arm. There was something caring in the way she handled him, the way she helped him. When their skin touched, she moaned a little and pressed her cunt against him. He grabbed her through her pants, could feel her heat, her wetness and it made him rigid. Normally Wade was more timid, allowing the women in his life to call the shots. Tonight, he was different. He was powerful and commanding, wanting nothing more than to fuck her like she deserved, like she needed.

He guided her to the bed where she fell on her back with a soft thump. This was not going to be a casual, missionary style fuck; he was going to make her beg for him.

Her eyes watched him with curiosity. In a series of quick movements, he stripped her of her boots, jeans, and panties. The light from the bedroom lamp bathed her in a soft glow. He rubbed the soft flesh of her belly and placed a gentle kiss. She squirmed, but settled down as he moved lower. He took off his belt, jeans, and boxers, letting his cock spring free.

"Uh uh," he said, "no peeking," as she moved to get a better look.

He placed a hand on her sternum and guided her back down on the bed. Her legs were spread wide, waiting for him. He stroked the length of his cock for several moments as he watched, taking in the sight of her. Her nipples, a ruddy pink, were already puckered. His eyes traveled lower. Her sex was delicate with neatly trimmed, dark blond hair.

"A blond, huh?" he said.

She laughed and her breasts bounced, "Don't tell anyone."

"I won't," he said as he knelt before her.

She was so wet, so tense in anticipation that she shivered at his hot breath on her skin. He liked the coppery smell of her. He spread her lips with his hand to reach her clit and licked her slowly, running his tongue from her clit to her hole and back again. With each stroke, her body shook and her hips arched toward his face.

Her chest rose and fell quickly. Her eyes were shut and her head tilted back. Soft moans escaped her lips, increasing in frequency. His lips formed a tight seal on her clit and as she began to buck, he thrust two of his fingers into her.

Her upper body came up off the bed and she came, screaming, a litany of "Oh god" and "Oh fuck" streaming from her lips.

Wade didn't give her much time to recover. "Roll over," he commanded, slapping her ass cheek hard enough to sting.

Grace groaned but did as she was told, resting her head on her folded arms. He ran his hands over her rounded ass that was now up in the air. Her back was also heavily tattooed—covered in koi fish and cherry blossoms swirling around a partially disrobed geisha. He swept her hair to the side so he could see all of it as he fucked her. On her lower back, he planted a series of gentle kisses. Her skin was silky and slightly salty.

"Tell me," he said as he slid a finger inside her tight opening, "do you like it from behind?"

"Yes," she nodded, shuddering from his ministrations.

"Oh, you're a dirty girl then," he said and laughed.

She was the perfect height, cunt open at exactly the right level for him. Wade hissed as he rammed his cock inside her in one deep thrust, knowing she was wet enough to take it. She cried out in pleasure, hands moving to grasp the blankets to steady herself.

Hands grabbing her hips, he pounded into her a couple of times and then withdrew, his cock hovering just inches from her. She tried to push back onto him, but he held her in place.

"Tell me you want it," he said as he slapped her ass cheek with his open hand.

She groaned and he slapped her flesh again.

"I want it," she said.

"Want what? I want you to say it," he rubbed her cunt with the tip of his cock. She was slick and hot with desire.

"I want your hard cock inside me. Now," she said.

He entered her again and she screamed, arching her back to meet him. He wanted to watch her ass rise and fall, trace the lines of her tattoos with his eyes, reach forward and grab a handful of her shiny black hair, but the pleasure was too much. He could only close his eyes, and lean his head back as he enjoyed the feeling of being inside her.

"You feel so good, so good," he repeated. It became a mantra of his pleasure.

She came twice, both times tearing at the bedding with her hands, burying her face to muffle her cries. He could feel the orgasms tear through her. It was so good to get her off, he wanted to last forever.

"C'mon baby," she panted as she drove herself back hard and fast. "Come for me."

He surrendered to her, to the sensation of her. His breathing quickened, his chest rising and falling as he moaned. Just as he was about to come, he pulled out, loosing his seed in sticky bursts on her ass.

His breath was ragged. She stood to face him. Her lipstick was smeared and her dark eye-makeup was in ruins. To Wade, she'd never looked more beautiful.

"That was hot," she said as she put her hands around his neck and kissed him deeply. "I've never been with a dirty talker before."

"I've never been one before," he shrugged. "I guess something just got into me."

"Well," she said, "I hope it stays." Her fingertips

grazed his chest. "I'm going to go clean up. Maybe you could grab us a cold drink from the fridge?"

Forgetting about the roommate, he headed down the hallway still nude. The apartment was dark. *I don't remember her turning off the lights,* he thought. He opened the fridge, light falling on his naked body as he leaned in to get a couple of cans of pop.

"Nice," he heard a female voice from behind him say.

He was so startled he dropped one of the cans from his grasp. It hit the linoleum floor with a thud and spun a few times. As he turned to face her, he recognized her immediately.

"Liv?"

"In the flesh," she replied. She wore a short, orange nightgown showing off her tiger tat. It was still a bit red but looked incredible.

"What are you—" he remembered his nakedness and quickly tried to cover himself with his free hand.

"…Doing here?" she finished. "We're roommates." She closed the gap between them. "Grace do that," she touched the edges of the medical tape still holding the cling film in place.

"Yeah."

She stood on her tiptoes to get a better look. She smelled like warm spices and a hint of patchouli. He hadn't even noticed that earlier. "Probably time to take that off. Grace'll clean it up for you. Guess it was too big for a pad."

He shifted from foot to foot, nervous about Grace coming out and finding him like this in front of Liv.

"Well," she smiled, "you should be getting color in

about two weeks. Maybe you can come back after and all three of us can play." She touched his cheek and peered into his eyes. "Grace and I share everything. Isn't that right, Grace," she said as she looked over her shoulder toward the darkened hallway.

Grace stood in the opening in a black satin robe that blended perfectly with her hair color. "That's right," she smiled. "But for now, I'm going to clean him up and get him to bed."

HER MIDNIGHT ROSES
BY ZAK JANE KEIR

MAC HEFTED THE NEW, VICIOUS FLOGGER with the knotted rubber tails and brought it down with a splashy crack on the arse of the woman he'd bent over the whipping bench. She yelped, then giggled, so he tried to make the next stroke harder and the third one harder than that. He liked screams, not giggles. The woman, a dumpy blonde whose name he'd already forgotten, let out a yelp that sounded a bit more like she was feeling it, and he swung again. The music playing in the background was some shitty grime or urban or whatever the fuck they called it, and it was putting him off, interfering with his ability to find his natural rhythm. He stepped back for a moment, shaking out the tails of the whip and glancing from side to side, wondering how much of an audience he had. There were a few men standing around and he got the impression they were watching him appreciatively, but he supposed they might have been just as enthralled by the blonde woman's naked backside, now bearing the marks of his skill. She had good skin, he'd say that for her, even if she was overweight.

He laid on the flogger again, delivering a succession

of blows fairly quickly, not particularly inclined to take his time over it. She'd been easy enough to pick up: too easy, really. She was probably desperate, and while he didn't mind a bit of desperation in a woman, he didn't see the need to use the likes of this one for any more than a quick warm up. There were plenty of other women in the place, and bound to be one or two who were sevens or higher while this one, even with her nice smooth skin, was never going to rate above a five. He didn't think he could even be bothered to make her suck him off once he'd finished flogging her.

Once she'd gone back to her giggling friends—and none of them were worth a second of his time or attention either—he made his way to the bar and ordered a glass of red. It didn't take long for a few of the betas, as he thought of them, to come flocking round, enthusiastic as usual, all gagging to find out if he had any new hints to offer on how to improve their chances of getting a bit of BDSM action of their own. A couple of them were keen to let him know they had actually made a cash donation to his website AlphaDom. It pleased him, though if they thought that would get them any extra tips that weren't available in his book, they had another fucking *think* coming. A beta was hardly ever capable of making it to alpha status, but there was no harm in giving them a bit of a boost from time to time. He didn't hide the fact that he'd been a bit of a beta in his younger days, but it was his looks that had lifted him up as much as the hard reading and hard work he'd put in on getting his game. Now he really was a master; master of the scene in so many ways. When he walked into a club, in his leather jeans and leather hat, people recognised him. People respected him, and there were always women who wanted more than just a look. He was the Alpha Dom.

Sure, there were still men neutered by feminism; men who actually claimed to like submitting to a woman. One had once cornered him for nearly half an hour to go on and on about the sub being the one in control of the scene. How it was totally acceptable to let some dumb bitch tie him up and even stick a butt plug up his arse, because it was all about getting his cock hard... No, thank you. When Mac's cock was hard, he'd get it sucked just the way he liked it.

He saw the redhead towards the end of the night, when he was coming back from the toilet. He looked at her for that beat too long, which was usually enough to attract any woman's attention, then looked away. For a moment he'd thought she might be a nine or even a ten: good pert tits, nice legs in stockings, little black rubber dress and a sweet-looking face, but then he'd seen her arms and mentally knocked her back down to a six. For a minute he'd thought the twining roses and brambles from wrists to shoulders were some sort of pattern on a skin-tight sheer top, but her dress was clearly sleeveless and all that decoration was in the form of tattooing. Only sluts had tattoos. Well, sluts and crazy fucking Goth girls who never shut up about their depression and their parents getting divorced. Then again, tattoos or no tattoos, she was still reasonably hot, and she seemed to be on her own. He looked again: she wasn't looking his way. His route back to the bar would take him fairly close to where she was standing, and he ran through his checklist of opening gambits on the grounds that she was bangable and apparently up for grabs. Then the fat blonde from a couple of hours ago came right up in his face with a couple of her friends behind her, wanting to know if he really was the guy who'd written that book. By the time he'd dealt with them all and got them to promise they'd never read it because it wasn't the sort of thing women needed to know about, the red-headed seven-eight-nine had disappeared. Mac decided it was time to call it a night.

***

Hannah had found a quiet corner at the far end of the bar, and was mentally beating herself up between gulps of cider. Why had she bent over for the guy in the black hat? It was pretty obvious he was an arrogant dickhead, pretty obvious that he had lost interest in her the minute he'd finished thrashing her, and she hadn't felt any of the kind of good connection she longed for even while he was doing it. She wouldn't even have minded a bit of humiliation play: she generally liked it, but somehow it just hadn't worked for her. It wasn't that she had any expectations of finding the perfect Master in one of the clubs: she wasn't sure she even wanted anything more than a bit of fun from time to time. It just seemed to be getting more and more difficult to get as much as that. She knew she was putting on a bit of weight, but she'd always heard and believed, that BDSM wasn't about looks as much as about attitude. These days, though, so many of the men on the scene seemed to be picking up the same toxic appearance-obsessed attitude as the mainstream world. Hannah sniffed, and swallowed back tears. She knew she ought to go and find Lily and Maria, but she just couldn't face them at the moment. Oh and now here came one of those pretty bitches who probably had the whole scene falling over itself to get at her: red hair, slim, gorgeous face and those amazing tattoos. Both the girl's arms were covered in this beautiful tangle of bramble cables and roses, some red, some pink, some purple and some black. Hannah found herself staring, and quickly looked away, but the redhead stopped in her tracks and Hannah's eyes were drawn back to her.

"It's all right," the girl said, and Hannah blushed, not even sure if it was her who was being addressed. "He's a sad, silly little man who needs to learn better manners. Don't let him get to you." Hannah blushed even harder—had this girl overheard the way Mr Alpha Dom had dismissed her? She was standing very close to Hannah now, and Hannah could see the beautiful detailing in her tattoos. The roses were so vividly drawn they almost seemed to move.

"My name's Di. Do you like my ink?" Hannah remembered just in time that 'ink' was what people with tattoos generally used to describe their decorated skin.

"It's beautiful. The roses are amazing."

Di smiled and put her hand on Hannah's arm. "You're fairly amazing yourself, you know," she said. Hannah opened her mouth and then closed it again, not sure what to say. She wasn't getting a particularly dominant vibe from this new acquaintance, but something inside her seemed to respond with surprising intensity. Di's fingertips were warm, her touch was light, but she wasn't removing her hand, and her eyes were wide and dark and seemed to offer something Hannah couldn't understand but knew she wanted. They carried on chatting, and Hannah had the impression it was pleasant and sociable and soothing to the raw parts of her soul, wounded by the Alpha Dom's contempt, but somehow she was losing track of what they were discussing.

"You need to come with me, now" Di said, her hand sliding swiftly and smoothly down Hannah's arm to entwine her fingers with Hannah's own. "It's almost midnight, come with me, this way."

They went back through the club, which was in the process of winding down with people beginning to take their leave of one another, but Hannah took very little notice. She felt shivery, almost brittle, as though one wrong word or wrong touch would make her shatter— or make her come. Di led her up the stairs and out through a door which opened onto the roof terrace. No one was there, and the full moon was almost directly above them. Hannah looked around, a part of her mind asking what on earth she was doing, but Di pushed her gently against the bare bricks of the surrounding wall and kissed her. Hannah returned the kiss, enthusiastically—she could do this. She could kiss and be kissed, and feel her body melting with pleasure. Di's tattooed arms were around her, holding her close, and the girl's leg was between Hannah's thighs, rubbing against her, grinding against her.

"You like my tattoos, don't you?" Di whispered against her lips. "Touch them, run your fingers over the pink roses, the pink ones, the pink ones."

Hannah looked down at the other girl's arms, and

saw the roses and the brambles shining and shifting in the moonlight.

What's happening to me? How did I get here, what is she doing? Di was holding her by the shoulders, so it was easy to caress her forearms, and Hannah wanted to touch the pink roses. They were so bright, so pretty, so warm as her fingers found them. Hannah gasped and choked and felt herself slamming back against the brickwork, coming and coming and she didn't quite know how, didn't quite know why. She was just coming, and all she could see was pink roses.

"What are you doing out here? We've been looking for you for ages, we thought you must have gone!" Maria stood in front of her, had grabbed her shoulder: Maria with her old raincoat on over the PVC minidress and trainers instead of her scarlet stilettos.

"I just needed a bit of air," Hannah said, smoothing down her skirt. "Sorry about that. Shall we walk, or get a cab?"

As they made their way out, Hannah told herself—and her friends—what a great night it had been. The quick play scene with that cocky dom bloke had been a bit of fun; he wasn't as brilliant as he thought he was but it had still been nice to have her arse warmed up. There would be other doms in the future, she was sure.

She was a bit tired, but it didn't matter: the odd image in her mind of a pink rose darkening to purple was just one of those random things that popped into her head. Perhaps it was one of the visuals they'd projected onto the screen at the far end of the dancefloor.

Half-asleep in the cab home, Hannah felt a good,

warm glow throughout her body and resolved to go clubbing more often.

***

Mac kept up with the general fetish scene gossip via a couple of Facebook groups and regular checks on Twitter, as well as the comments section of his own website—though a lot of the latter consisted of removing the bullshit and insults that came in from what he generally thought of as manginas and feminazis—scum who didn't understand the way the world really worked and hated him for telling the truth. Women were there to be mastered, conquered and taken and they fucking loved it when they met a real man who knew how to treat them. Part of the problem with the world was the lack of men with the guts to take what they were created to take, to be the men they ought to be. He was doing his best to show them what they could do and what they could become, and his book and his website were bringing him in a decent income, but there were still so many people who just didn't get what he was trying to do. He had his subscribers, and his books were selling, and getting recognised was a good thing, on the whole. Yeah, once in a while someone would call him a prick, and there had been that one girl in the Scottish club who had dumped a drink over him and tried to kick him in the balls—he'd been able to get the bouncers to throw her out, but he hadn't felt like sticking around himself afterwards.

Recently, he'd found himself pulling ahead of his rivals, in terms of book sales and mentions on other sites, which should have felt amazing, particularly as some of them seemed to have pretty much disappeared over the last year or so. Instead, it made him feel ill at ease and unsettled. He'd been doing his best to dismiss the rumours that were circulating on sections of Reddit and 4chan that certain big players were announcing a change of heart and talking about respecting women. Others had just gone, their profiles taken down, emails to them bouncing back with no explanation. Of course, there were a few betas and even a wannabe Alpha claiming that feminists might have murdered the likes of IncelWarrior42 and DominatorPaul, two previously prolific contributors to discussions. Incel had apparently made some reference to a woman who was stalking him shortly before deleting his account. Mac's own thoughts were that Incel had shut down his old account and started a new one—hadn't several of them told him that a name like that was going to drag him down? Mac had quite a following among the Incel communities, though he sometimes wondered whether it was worth the effort of being polite to the ones that came across as gammas or deltas, not even betas. Yeah, Mac remembered what it was like being incel—involuntarily celibate—but he wasn't going to advertise the fact, for fuck's sake. That was a shortcut to losing your game completely: if you told women you were a failure they'd laugh in your face, and there was no need to stay a failure, anyway.

It was Saturday morning, and he was planning to hit House of Sins that night: there were always plenty of women there. It was one of the flashier, dress-up clubs so you got the girls who thought the kink scene would be exciting but didn't have a clue, and even the fours and fives made the effort with their outfits, so there was bound to be something to bang. He'd gone online to announce his intentions—well, not to be too specific about which club he was planning on honouring in case some Social Justice Warrior arsehole decided to come after him and make a big noise about it to the point that the club wouldn't let him in. OK, that hadn't happened so far and probably wouldn't while he carried on using that line drawing he'd picked up rather than a photograph of himself as his avatar. No point in taking chances, though. As it was, a lot of the online chatter was about another disappearance, and Mac was surprised to realise that it was someone he actually knew. SmartPhil was one of the few of Mac's followers who seemed to be able to put Mac's theories into practice; Mac had seen the guy get a woman bent over in a club more than once.

Mac did a search, followed a few threads, but couldn't find much in the way of hard information. Of course, people were bringing up IncelWarrior42 and the others who had gone or changed their tune dramatically, and airing their pet theories all over again: SJW infiltrators, feminist sympathisers, even a Government conspiracy to neuter or eliminate men who understood the way of the world. What did come up more than once was that SmartPhil had said something about a woman following him or meeting a woman who was different, and that he'd mentioned a woman with tattoos—and now people were saying that Incel had been threatened by a girl who had "some freaky shit tattoos, he said, she was a nutter, maybe she's a serial killer, some crazy feminazi cunt, maybe we're all in danger."

Mac winced, some odd memory surfacing that he couldn't quite put into words. He didn't like tattoos on women, so why was he having this sudden mental image of tattooed arms reaching out to him, and it arousing him? He read through a few more posts of an impassioned discussion of whether or not the posters would bang 'a bitch with ink' before getting bored and deciding to phone for a pizza.

***

Di, whose real name was something most people would struggle to pronounce, paid the usual close attention to her appearance. She was sticking with the Goth look this time around as it was proving highly effective. Some environments, some situations, she wore a dress or other item of clothing with a pattern of roses: on occasion she had woven the roses into a wreath to crown herself. Wearing them on her skin was perhaps her favourite method of using them though. She stood looking at herself in the old silver mirror, admiring the black velvet basque and midnight blue shorts. Fishnet tights and big boots completed the look, and her long red hair was wound in a tight plait. The roses and brambles twining around her arms were now almost all black, with just one still a deep, dark red.

She heard a car pulling up outside: the minicab had arrived. Di smiled at her reflection, picked up her long black coat and left the room. She understood the Alpha Dom much better than he understood himself, and tonight it was his turn to increase his understanding.

***

House of Sins was busy, as usual. Mac had done a couple of circuits of the place, scoping out what was worth banging, and spotted several possibilities. There were at least four eights in there, though two of them looked like they'd be too much trouble to detach from the men they were with. There were also plenty of fours, who might serve to make the eights—and the seven he'd just spotted—competitive. Mind you, it might be worth making a start on the seven: aim high, he'd always told himself. Aim high and bang higher: he grinned, and began to make his way towards her, mentally listing her merits. Dark blonde hair, probably natural; very nice tits showed off in a red rubber dress that was cut good and low. She looked at him, and then looked away and Mac thought: yes, you're interested. He was within about three feet of her when some other woman—no more than a three or four at most, rushed at the blonde, squealing excitedly, squealing like the pig she was, and the seven squealed back and they started hugging each other like teenagers. Mac detoured smoothly away: he might come back later or he might not. High-rating women with a lot of low-rating female friends were sometimes more trouble than they were worth: being the only good-looking woman in a gang of heifers tended to make a woman too arrogant.

It was getting on for midnight when Mac went down to the bar for what he had decided was going to be his final drink. For some reason, the night was turning out to be more frustrating than usual, so it would probably be best to go home rather than hang around till the bitter end like the desperate betas sometimes did. Any women not picked up by the end of the night were either ugly as shit or crazy. He was just about to take the first sip when he felt a light touch on his arm, and turned to see a petite redhead smiling up at him.

"I think we might have met before," she said. "How's your night going?" Mac couldn't speak at first: having a woman approach him was a rare thing and one he didn't normally like. This one was pretty, and she did look familiar, and when he looked her over he reckoned that she was a high eight or maybe a nine. The tattoos, though… Why did women fucking do that to themselves, did they think it made them interesting or special? He was going to brush her off and walk away, but her hand was still resting on his arm and he realised his cock had stiffened, was incredibly, almost frighteningly hard. He couldn't take his eyes off those tattoos, those black roses twined round her arms.

"It's getting better," he said, and gave her the smile he'd practised so many times. "Maybe it's about to get better for both of us."

"Yes," she said, "I think you're right. How about we go to the Upper Room? It's nearly midnight."

Mac followed her, admiring the way she slipped through the crowd, admiring the wiggle of her pert bottom in those shorts, grinning in eager anticipation. His mind felt a little foggy, but he didn't really care: he was focussed on the promise of those lovely buttocks. The Upper Room was the section of the club where people went to get a lot more down and dirty than was permitted in the rest of the venue, and men were only allowed past the red velvet curtain if they were accompanied by a woman. Some people loved the space, Mac had heard; others were less enthusiastic about the idea of any explicit, blatant sexual activity taking place on club premises. He thought it would be no bad thing for others to see him getting his cock sucked by a girl like this. He'd overlook the tattoos, he decided, seeing as the rest of her was so hot.

In fact, the Upper Room was empty. A tiny part of him wondered about that: normally it was supposed to be heaving around midnight, but the redhead smiled at him again and then ran her tongue slowly over her lips.

"I'm going to suck you now," she said. "I'm going to suck you like you've never been sucked before." She backed him up against a pillar in the furthest corner of the room, and Mac groaned aloud, his cock rigid and aching as she undid his trousers and delved inside. His leather jeans slid down, down past his knees, almost to his ankles, and she stood up and kissed him, and took a pair of handcuffs from her belt.

Cuffs? She'd fastened one round his left wrist before he'd really understood what she was doing, and he almost panicked, but she kissed him again, and it was somehow OK, somehow it didn't matter all that much as she guided his other hand behind his back, behind the pillar. There was a soft but audible click as the second cuff locked, and Mac was trapped in place, bound upright, unable to escape.

She knelt in front of him and those perfect pouting lips of hers closed over his cockhead, and her tongue began to lash around his shaft.

"Oh god, yeah" he gasped, throwing back his head and closing his eyes. He'd never felt anything so intense in his life, and he realised he wanted to look at her while she took him with her mouth. She was taking him… it was amazing and strange to be in such a position. He looked down at her, saw the crown of her head bobbing up and down, saw the roses on her arms and wondered why he had thought tattoos were ugly. These were beautiful and he wanted to touch them, to stroke her arms as she pleasured him. He couldn't move his hands, though. He couldn't touch her.

She slowly eased his cock from between her lips and stood again, smiling at him. He was incredibly hard, aware of a pulsing trickle of fluid leaking from the head of his cock. She took a step back and then reached out for him with her rose-covered arms, moving right up close again, wrapping herself around him and holding him tight. Her skin was so hot it was almost burning, and suddenly Mac was seeing things he had tried not to see, tried not to remember…the contemptuous smile of a woman he'd tried to hit on, the anguished eyes of the many girls he'd treated with unkindness or disdain ever since, those rare—very rare—moments of mutual pleasure that he'd somehow briefly found.

The girl slithered down his body and now her lips were round his shaft again, her arms around his thighs, and his mind was breaking into utter incoherence. She sucked him with avid determination, and he could hardly stand it.

"I'm going to come! I'm going to come, babe, please, let me come!' He thought he heard her laugh, and then she sucked him even harder, rubbing his balls with her fingertips, and taking him deep and he was coming then, coming in great gouts and spasms, and she swallowed it all down and it seemed as though all he could see was roses, so many roses, turning from black and dark purple to a warm and tender shade of red.

His hands were loose by his sides, and there were tears on his face. He shook his head, dazed, and realised his trousers were still round his ankles. He pulled them up, fastened them, looked around him. The Upper Room was empty, so he made his way down the stairs: there were a few final stragglers propping up the bar but he ignored them. Making his way towards the exit, he found himself thinking what a fucking idiot he'd been for the last few years, so bitter, so stupid. He was going to take down his website, delete his accounts, pull his book from Amazon, grow up and get a fucking life. That was what he was going to do.

Di licked her lips as she made her way home. That one had been interesting. More than interesting: quite delicious, in fact. On her arms, the roses seemed to throb and pulsate, and she hugged herself, running her hands up and down her heated, sated skin. This game could continue forever.

NINE LIVES
BY HARLEY EASTON

TRINA MONROE KNEW SHE DIDN'T LOOK like much to the outside world, and she was fine with that. In fact, she preferred it. Being ignorable meant more time doing what she loved and less time doing, well, things like she'd been doing most of the day. She peeked out of the green room and into the Expo Hall praying it was empty and that she looked as nondescript as possible. Considering the convention, she was so normal as to be practically invisible.

Most of her stringy hair was stuffed under a hat. Trina wasn't willing to fight with it at this point in the day. The few tendrils that spilled out were the same pale lilac they'd been for the last decade, long before it ever became popular. Under her oversized sweater jacket, tank top, and jeans was a relatively toned but non-athletic body of generally average height and shape. Makeup was something other people messed with. By all accounts she was pretty but plain, and she didn't really care.

Unfortunately for her, to those in the know, Trina Monroe was the most desirable woman in the building.

With twenty years in the business, Trina was one of the hottest tattoo artists in the country. She'd bested even the strongest male artists in a field that was still dominated by misogynistic garbage. There was no disputing she was a rock star in her profession, and she'd gotten her fame by hard work and exceptional talent, not by selling out to some reality show.

I just don't get pandering to the media to make a career. Trina had seriously debated even coming to the weekend's activities. Her business partner and long-time friend, Josh, had convinced her that she needed to share her knowledge with the new wave of tattoo artists. *When your mentor says something like that, you suck it up and do it,* Trina admonished herself. After all, Josh had given her a shot when hardly anyone would hire a female, let alone one eighteen and completely untrained. Despite his nagging the last few years, Trina had avoided the requests to speak about her art. When the Portland invite came, he'd filled out the paperwork for her.

"You don't even have to travel," Josh had pestered her once the presenter packet came back and she'd tossed it on his desk. It wasn't like she wanted the publicity; Trina was more than busy enough. The repeat clients she worked with because she liked them. The celebrities she worked with because they paid stupid amounts to have her tattoo them with an original piece. Luckily, she was past the point of dealing with drunken customers getting inked with inevitable regrets and college kids wanting rebellion more than art. It was no small blessing to be successful enough to be selective.

Lectures were done for the day. The eleven o'clock was a three-person panel to discuss stylization and reproducing complex imagery from classic works of art. The room had been overflowing with people. At two, another rather large crowd had gathered to hear her ideas about evolving their own artistic style with depth and flow techniques. The panels had actually been fun, almost invigorating. She was rejuvenated by the ideas being tossed back and forth by artists at the top of their game. What sapped her reserves right back to zero was all the people.

They were everywhere and each one wanted something from her. After both panels, she'd been mobbed by requests to be put on a waiting list. She'd maneuvered out of the crowd only for a conversation staffer to rush her to a meet and greet table where people asked individually instead of en masse. It'd been rewarding hearing so much admiration for her work, but Trina was ready to be done with people for the day. For her, the art was a much more intimate thing.

Glancing into the Expo Hall, she saw a few stragglers dashing into the ballroom. With most of the attendees at the party and end of day art show, Trina figured she was clear to make a quick exit. Just as she was about to escape, a question came from behind her.

"Trina? Trina Monroe?" The voice was soft, apologetic, and distinctly male. Trina sighed, rolled her eyes and turned to face whoever it was that wanted one more thing from her.

He was muscular; that was plainly visible through the long-sleeved gray shirt that managed to both cover and expose him. It glossed over his rippled pecs and massive arms like it had been painted on. His hands were stuffed into the pockets of his tan cargo pants. Hunched shoulders suggested he was expecting rejection, but his baby face held an expression of hope beneath the rich brown stubble on his chin. Unruly hair poked out from under a beanie cap, and his only visible tattoos were a tiny cat on the inside of his right wrist and a tiger pattern hiding just beneath the left sleeve of his shirt. The whole package was unbelievably sexy.

It's also just not enough at this point in the day. Trina was done being nice, so she folded her arms and leaned back giving him a hard look. "Something I can do for you?"

"I just…" It seemed difficult for him to get the words out, but Trina waited. When she didn't walk away he shook himself, stood straighter, and looked her dead in the eye. "I wanted to say thank you."

"For?" Her arms loosened a bit. The man was about her age, a little younger maybe. The longer he stood there, the more Trina thought he looked familiar. It'd be easy to dismiss him as a convention attendee; she'd certainly seen plenty of people today. Somehow she knew that wasn't how she knew him, and it nagged at her.

"I doubt you remember me. You did my first three pieces." Now that the words were flowing his confidence seemed to grow. "I really can't explain how much they've meant to me."

"Really?" Trina's arms slipped entirely as she assessed the man before her. *It couldn't be*, she thought. With all the people she'd seen over the years, all the new and repeat customers, she still hoped she was right. The hope made her hesitant. Still she asked, "Can I see?"

His face lit with relief. He pushed his left sleeve up a little higher and displayed his forearm. A tribal style tiger looked back at her with soulful eyes. "When I heard you were going to be here I knew I had to get a ticket. When I got called in today I was worried I'd miss you."

Without thinking, Trina grasped his arm and ran her fingers over the ink. The drawing was far simpler than her recent work, obviously from her earlier days. "Leo," she whispered, feeling for the scars she knew were covered beneath the ink. His arm jerked a bit in her hands.

"You really remember?"

I've never forgotten, she thought. That kid had grabbed a piece of her young heart and never let it go. Not that she had admitted it when they were younger. She was too busy trying to prove herself then, and she'd kicked herself hard when he left.

Rather than answer, Trina moved her fingers to hover just over his heart. There, she traced an odd pattern, invisible beneath his clothes, but one she knew was there all the same. "Leonard Novak, you've been gone a very long time."

He wrapped her in a hug which she gratefully sank into. Trina had indeed done Leo's first tattoo, and she remembered painstakingly designing the tiger stripes to cover the self-harm scars that littered his forearm at the time. The soulful eyes had been her way of reminding him never to cut himself again. It had been nearly fifteen years since her friend had been in Portland and she'd always wondered what had happened. He'd started as a skinny kid and evolved to a fairly athletic twenty-something before he'd disappeared. But there was a lot of time to cover between that boy and this buff god.

"Well, I'm back in the area now. Tried about two years ago to contact my friend Katrina and see if she'd be willing to ink me again, but now that she's some big time artist she can't fit a guy in."

Trina giggled and playfully beat him on the chest, then leaned back and smiled. "A guy should have mentioned he was an old friend." That earned her a hearty belly laugh.

"Apparently everyone says that. I got an earful from Josh. Wouldn't even let me give him my name, but he did call me more than a few colorful terms before hanging up."

"He's learned to be protective." Trina paused, wondering if she was going to regret what she was about to do then deciding she didn't care. "Still looking for some art?"

Leonard raised a brow. "From the famous Trina Monroe?"

"Consider it catching up with an old friend. I've got a studio area in the back of my house. You could come over, catch me up on the past ten years, show me what you've had done. I could at least sketch you something," Trina bit her lip, imagining Leo shirtless in her home. Stopping herself from hoping it might go anywhere she continued. "If you like it, maybe I could start the lines tonight."

"How could I turn down an offer like that?" His hand slid to the small of Trina's back as he escorted her to the parking lot and they drove to her house.

*****

"Nice place," Leo had been chilling on her sofa for almost an hour. The conversation had picked up like he'd never left, like he was the same twenty year old that had spent his time hanging around at Josh's studio. Much like then, he was all questions and very few explanations. It had always taken Leo a bit to warm up, to uncurl that knot of emotions he tried to hide. Trina decided to call him on it just like she used to.

"Cut the small talk, Novak," she said as she came back from the kitchen with a couple of beverages. Trina tossed him a can of cola, which he easily caught. Popping hers open, she took a drink before giving him an exaggerated leer. "You're here for one reason pretty boy. Strip."

For all his seeming confidence, Leo managed a blush as he braced his hands on his knees to stand. Trina couldn't resist kidding him "What's the matter? Have a problem showing off my work?"

"No. Just showing off to you." He was standing in front of the couch now, his hand running along the back side of his neck and his gaze falling anywhere but on her.

"Wh... What?" she stuttered. She was the invisible girl, the one with a smart mouth, great talent, and no tattoos of her own. It had taken years to cultivate the careful look of plain and ordinary so people would take her work seriously. *How can that boy I always cared*

about, this impeccably sculpted god before me, be nervous?
she marveled.

He didn't respond. Instead, he pulled his shirt off
over his head and began kicking off his shoes and socks.
The gasp that escaped her when he dropped his pants
was covered by the rustling of the fabric. At least, she
hoped it was. If Leo heard it, he made no sign and he
said nothing as he stood clad only in a pair of blue
boxer briefs and his ink.

The artwork covered a good portion of his torso and
varying parts of his legs. Slowly, he turned to show her
every piece. After the second rotation, she reached out
a trembling hand that stopped him, despite the fact she
was still several steps away. Timidly, Trina approached
and clasped his forearm, once again running her fingers
over the delicate designs of the tribal tiger. Leo let out
a ragged breath, shuddering but otherwise remaining
still.

"Eighteen. Your first. You wanted it a year before,
but I knew what the scars were and wouldn't agree to
ink you unless you stopped hurting yourself." It had
been those scars that first tugged at her heart, and his
stubborn persistence, coming in the shop every other
month for the full year, that had won it completely.
He'd been skinny and completely flawed, but no less
attractive than he was right now.

Leo nodded, but, again, did not respond. Trina let
her fingers gloss over the curve of his bicep. Instead of
lingering on the bulging muscle or the striking
definition, her hands found their way over to a massive
lion head tattoo that covered his left pec from shoulder
to stomach. Ignoring the delicacy of the face and the

mixture of colors in the flowing mane, she moved toward his heart, where there was a small star. She traced the tiny points of the pattern then followed an invisible line connecting that star to several others, obscured but still visible beneath the bold but somber portrait of the great cat.

"Twenty. Your second. You'd been hanging out at the studio in your spare time." *God, how I loved every day you came in, and how it hurt me when you asked for this one*, she remembered as she took a breath before continuing. "The bruises below your ribs were healing so I didn't want to do the work. You convinced me. Your step-father had been beating you on a regular basis after he saw the first tattoo." Trina's face twisted in pain at her words. "I didn't know."

"I hid it pretty well," Leo agreed.

"From your mother and sister too," Trina noted. "You told me you needed to know that there was more and that you were connected to it. So we came up with it together, the stars in the Leo constellation."

Leo nodded. When she continued to trace the pattern he shifted, looking down at her as he clenched and unclenched his fists. "I left the house that week. Walked out without a word. I owed him *nothing*."

"Left the studio too." That had hurt, not nearly as bad as what he'd done later, but she'd felt his absence every day he'd avoided them that year. "Only came in every once in a while after that until you showed up for the overlay."

"I needed to build my strength. I asked for a real lion this time. Had to get my head out of the clouds. I owed that much to mom and Silvia. I should have been looking out for them instead of myself. I would have been able to protect them when..."

"When you found out he was beating them instead." Leo's breathing sped up and he twitched at the memory, so Trina continued. "I missed you when you left," she whispered. Wanting to calm him, and wanting something else she didn't dare contemplate, Trina dared placing a single kiss on the brightly colored swirl of mane that graced his shoulder.

The reaction was immediate. Leo's massive hands grasped her shoulders, tenderly holding her with her palms pressed against his chest and her head pulled away. "Don't," he whispered. "Please don't unless..."

"Unless what, Leo?" Trina searched his face, but it was closed.

In a moment he gently pushed her away gently and sat down on the couch, reaching for his pants. "This was a bad idea," he grumbled.

"Wait. Please," she pleaded, and for some reason, he did. The pants remained on the floor, but Leo ran his hands over his face in obvious frustration. Trina took her time walking over. She approached him as she would a wounded animal. When she sat next to him on the couch her hand fell on his left thigh just above the knee. It was a much smaller image, only about the size of a palm, and much less macho than the rest. The artist had done a simple silhouette of two small black cats resting on tree branch, their backs facing outward, their unseen faces turned to witness an abstract of a colorful sunset. "This one?"

"I ended up moving us to Boston to get away from…" Leo gritted his teeth and took a breath before continuing. "Thought I could keep Mom and Sil safe there. Then they got in a car wreck. When I got to the hospital, mom put her hand right there and told me everything would be fine. I knew she was lying."

Trina cursed under her breath. As if spurred on, Leo flashed his right wrist where she could see a white inked tattoo of a kitten with a halo. "Same year, my girlfriend decided to abort our kid. Didn't tell me until weeks afterward when I found her leaving the apartment. I might have gotten a little reckless after that."

The thought of that loss made her ache for him, but Leo didn't give her much time to process. He moved right along, pointing at his right calf where a cheetah stood growling and clearly in mid-twitch with its tail. "Ran into a burning house down the street before the firemen could get there. I couldn't let that family lose their kid."

They're all cats, she realized. Every single one of his tattoos was a feline reminder of some of the worst moments in his life. Leo had told her the painful story behind seven. The drawing was already formulating in her mind. Trina knew what she would give him if he let her, but she wouldn't go there until she knew about the last one. She crawled above him, balancing on the back of the sofa with her feet pressed against his hips and her knees against his arms.

"And this?" she asked, placing both her hands on his shoulders and running her palms down his back. Leo smirked and looked over his shoulder at her.

"That's the one I wanted you to do." The panther face was well rendered. *I wonder if I know the artist,* she mused briefly. Like the rest of his art, the figure displayed a somber, graceful strength. Also like several of his tattoos, scars were hidden beneath the image. "I got all my stuff in Boston done by the same guy. Brody was pretty cool; hung around the mixed martial arts studio where I taught. Told me once that Boston was a great town, but apparently not for me. While he inked the cheetah he said he'd never seen luck like mine and I might be better off somewhere else. I kinda laughed it off, you know."

"Mm-hmmm," she hummed. Trina doubted she could have laughed after all he'd been through. Just hearing about it all made her ache for what he'd lost. Her index finger thoughtfully copied the line of the solemn, almost human eyes of the panther over and over again before her thumbs followed the curve of his shoulder blade up to his neck.

"My studio wasn't in a great area. Brody and I were breaking up fights all the time. One day, we stop this group of punks from beating up some kid on the street. I guess they recognized us because that night, they surprised me when I was unlocking the studio. One of them had a knife. When Brody picked me up from the ER, he said Boston wasn't home for me anymore. I came back here."

"I'm glad you did," Trina murmured. Leo went quiet then, his breath slowing with her soothing motions as she rubbed his shoulders. After a few minutes he reached up to touch her hand and Trina stilled. Trying to lighten the mood she nudged him with her knee as she bent down over his shoulder. "I think this is the most you've ever spoken to me at once."

Leo turned and kissed her. It was bittersweet, filled with loss and longing, but tender. For what could have been minutes or hours, he pressed his lips to hers, never pressing on until she opened her mouth to gasp for air; his tongue moved to explore her further. His body twisted around as he knelt up on the couch without breaking the kiss. When he finally pulled away, Trina was dizzy. She opened her eyes to find him staring at her with mix of awe and need. She smirked even as she blushed. "More a man of action, huh?"

He lunged forward, pinning her to the wall with his second kiss as they both tore at her sweater jacket. His massive hands pushed up under her top, roaming along her waist then up to her breasts. Trina leaned forward long enough to rip it off over her head and reached to pull Leo back toward her.

His possessive mouth came down to claim her nipple, his tongue swirling around the pink circle of her areola before his teeth nipped playfully at the tip. Her fingers gripped the top of the couch and as her hips canted forward, Leo wasted no time guiding her legs around his waist. Once her lower limbs were wrapped around him, he moved to her other breast. Trina gasped at the assault, making Leo raise his head to study her face.

"More," she murmured. The word brought a wicked grin. He shifted his massive arms beneath hers and cradled her shoulders before lifting her off the couch. If he expected her to loosen her legs from their perfect perch above his hips, he was mistaken. Trina clung to his skin as closely as any tattoo. Leo sunk back down on the couch and she moved just enough to straddle him. Through her jeans Trina could feel him hard and ready beneath her.

She recognized the moment for what it was. He wanted her, needed her, but he was letting her do this on her terms; Leo would not take advantage of her. Swiftly, she pulled off her jeans and panties, and leaned forward to rip off the boxer briefs that barely contained him. She only got them as far down as his knees before she straddled him again impatiently. Using her hand to slide him along her wetness, she lined up and felt his thickness inside her.

It took a moment to adjust to his girth; it'd been too long since Trina had even thought about bringing someone home. Leo gave her the time, using it to run his hands through her hair and stroke gentle patterns across her skin. When she began moving, he shuddered, leaned his head back, and growled. The sound was full of ecstasy; it reverberated in his chest, seeming to come from the lion splayed across his pec. Even as Trina braced her palm on the beautiful drawing, Leo brought his hands down to frame her hips.

With every thrust, he pushed deeper inside her, and she let him. Trina wanted to protect him, to heal him. She wanted to fuck away all the pain he'd felt and remove every scar concealed beneath the artwork he'd used to hide himself. Leo moved one hand to cup her ass and brought the other hand around between them. When his thumb brushed her clit, her body arched and she cried out with pure pleasure. He began working her then, rubbing slowly but roughly, seeming to know the perfect rhythm for her need.

Her head jerked forward and she opened her eyes to find him staring at her. She could feel the throb of his cock inside her. Leo was soaking up her pleasure, reveling in the waves of bliss rolling over her face and making her body quake. But soon, his face contorted, his thumb sped up and his hips stopped rising to meet hers.

"Katrina," his voice was ragged. "I can't... I need to satisfy you."

She slammed her hips down to take him in fully, writhing atop him and grinding their bodies together. Within seconds, she heard him groan and felt him let go inside her. The glorious pressure combined with the movement of his thumb pushed Trina to climax. She trembled above him, letting the sensations rip through her as she fell forward, cloaking them both with her lavender hair.

They panted, clinging to each other on the couch as he grew soft inside her. Trina kissed Leo on the cheek before moving off him and grabbed a blanket from a nearby chair. She tossed him the blanket and reached for her jacket, still bunched on the top of the couch behind him.

"That was... unexpected," he finally settled on, struggling for words.

"Really?" Trina asked coyly as she slipped the jacket on and pulled it around her. Leo nodded, suddenly shy again.

"I've wanted you for a very long time, Kat."

The phrase hit Trina right in the chest. After the shock faded a bit, warmth flooded her body. *All those years hanging around the studio and he never said a word,* she thought. The only thing she said was, "still interested in that artwork?"

Leo stayed quiet. Trina realized she was going to have to get used to that. She ran into the next room and grabbed a sketch pad and pens. When she came back, Leo was pulling on his pants. She slid in front of him, placing her palm on his abs, and gave him a kiss on his still bare chest before softly pushing him back to sitting on the couch. Then, she sat on the opposite side, braced her feet on his thigh, and put the sketch pad on her knees, sitting there as casually as if they'd done this every evening for years.

Trina talked to him as she sketched. Leo rarely answered with more than a caress on her foot or leg. The sketch took some time, as the eventual tattoo would. After a while, Trina lowered the sketch pad and found Leo asleep sitting up. She smiled and finished her drawing.

The sketch was a cat, of course: a silky black feline with a gentle face and a feminine body. Her human form was cloaked in a toga that split in the middle, displaying shapely legs. Egyptian jewelry dripped from her neck, waist, and ankles. Her hands were cupped before her, protecting a glowing heart. Trina knew that Bast, feline goddess and protector, would shield Leo and his future, but for now she would protect his heart. Gently, she woke her slumbering lion, and led him to bed.

THE VORON-KALI EMPEROR'S NEW CLOTHES

BY GREGORY L. NORRIS

I.

MORE COLOR, MORE MAGIC. Adam's needle, already an extension of his fingers—which were an extension of his soul and imagination, filled in blank space, transforming skin to artwork.

The project had started on the former soldier's feet—Heidelberg Man on the left, Nebraska Man on Luke's right. The rest of the subjects of The Evolution of Man, from Piltdown through Peking, Neanderthal to Cro-Magnon, had steadily marched up his customer's legs, past hairy shins to thighs. Modern Man was presently only half there, a ghost whose silhouette was sketched over Luke's erection. The ghost walked upright and, for a shocking instant, seemed to gaze back at him through vacant eyes.

Adam Valico froze. From his position beside the naked man, with Luke's stiff cock in his grip, a strange emotion crept over his flesh, cool and tempestuous at the same moment. He glanced down to see all of

Mankind's past participants staring back from the canvas of the man's anatomy. The combined smell of ink, blood, and Luke's sweat threatened to possess him. Choking down a dry swallow, Adam stroked the cock in his grip, lying to himself that the tug was designed to keep his customer hard. Luke was already under the influence of two sonam elixirs to block the pain and living out an untold number of fantasies beneath the dream glasses over his eyes.

"A perfect analogy," said a man's voice.

At first, Adam thought one of the ancestors of Modern Man had spoken. He turned his head to see a stranger standing inside the curtain of his workspace. "This is a private studio. Get out."

The man didn't. Instead, he strutted in without invitation, picked up one of the metal chairs lined along the wall, and took it backwards, assuming the pose of Old Earth cowboys, police detectives, and other confident tough guys. With the ex-soldier's cock pulsing in his hand, his stylus in the other, Adam quickly recorded the newcomer's details—more than a few years on him, rugged, attractive, eyes gray, like a wolf's. Another shamed refugee from the former Earth Expansion Militia, he guessed.

"No, I'm not E.E.M.," the man said.

"So, you're a mind reader?"

"Not minds, no. Statistics, body language, theoreticals."

Adam sucked down a deep breath. The strange emotion was back, and this time it sat mostly cold upon his epidermis. "You're a Mage?"

The man expressed his answer with a shrug and

through the waving fingers of one hand.

"You're all supposed to be dead. Extinct—"

"So was the Coelacanth, but they kept showing up in fishing nets off the coast of Madagascar on our Mother-world."

"—the first casualty of the Voron-Kali Blitz."

"That first loss would have been the majority of our space defense fleet."

Adam met the other man's eyes, determined not to blink first. "What do you want?"

The Mage said, "I come in search of the finest skin artist in the Occupied Colonies and see you holding the future of the human race in your hands."

Adam blinked against his will. His eyes wandered back to his customer's hard cock, now leaking pre-come around the pressure of his grip, and the vision of Homo sapiens, an apparition barely there. "What?"

"We need your help."

"We?"

"Piltdown Man, New Guinea Man…especially Modern Man. All that came before and might follow us in the days ahead, because, without you, the human race will end there, unfinished."

The Mage tipped his wolfish gray eyes down at the customer's cock, which began to unload in Adam's hand.

II.

Adam entered his hovel and suffered a rush of embarrassment at the condition of the place—plates left in the sink, piles of clothes in need of laundering, and the sweaty-sock funk that hung over the single oblong room.

"Don't worry, I'm not here to give housekeeping tips," the Mage said.

Adam answered with a humorless laugh while latching the deadbolt. "If you'd sent an official communiqué, I could have tidied up and put on the teakettle."

"This will do, as is," the Mage said.

The other man picked up a pair of dirty socks abandoned beside the bed where Adam slept, raised them to his nose, and inhaled. Then, to Adam's continued surprise, the Mage fondled the bulge in the front of his pants.

"What are you reading from that?" Adam asked.

"The future."

Adam made a face. "Wouldn't tea leaves be more precise...and less fragrant?"

The Mage smiled, and Adam indulged in acknowledging how handsome his visitor was. Painfully so, in fact. The longer he looked, the more his attraction burned.

"So, what do my sweaty socks tell you about the future?"

"A lot."

The Mage stood and guided Adam over to the mirror, an oval of smudged glass from a broken dresser frame now fixed to the wall. Adam faced his reflection, seeing himself for the millionth time. And also the first.

"In one possible outcome, you and I will do amazing things together."

Adam's hair, black and spiky on top, his sapphire

eyes, slender body, presently dressed in black tank top and cargo pants, and old boots, looked fresher, somehow newer. He wondered if he was gazing at the familiar through the Mage's wolf's eyes.

"We will create the means in which to defeat the Voron-Kali and to liberate our Mother and her colonial children from the invaders."

Adam's tattoos seemed to glow in this trance of second sight. The smiling sundial sun over his right shoulder ignited, warming the plethora of colorful planets cascading over biceps and wrists, spilling onto the back of his hand, past bottom knuckles—Earth, Planet Xanadu, the Elysian Fields, and the Bailey-Vortiss Archipelago of Planets. All of the former E.E.M. realm, now subjugated as property by the Voron-Kali Empire.

"The last of our defense fleet waits to strike," the Mage said. "But while their combined might would inflict decent casualties on those multi-cocked horrors from Orion's Arm, they'd ultimately be overwhelmed. A million men and a thousand heavy cruisers cannot do the job, but one man—one *artist*—might."

Adam listened. The Mage lifted his shirt. The skin of Adam's chest crackled with invisible electricity. The sun and planets jumped off his flesh and into the air around him as the Mage's fingers found the tiny hard points of his nipples and pinched. The front of Adam's pants swelled. The Mage unbuckled his belt, unbuttoned his fly, reached in. Adam moaned as the concentric ripples of pleasure ramped up, consuming the rest of his anatomy.

"One man?" Adam asked, his voice falling into the

cosmic waves, reaching his ear with a dreamy echo.

"An artist," the Mage said. "One who mixes his own paints, grinds his own pigments, like the noble calligraphists of Ancient Japan…"

The Mage's nostrils brushed his neck. Inhales followed, intimate and adding to Adam's excitement. Then the other man kissed his way down Adam's spine. The Mage appeared in front of him, freeing cock and balls, the latter so full, so *loose*, that Adam imagined them spilling all the way down to his hairy ankles. But as the Mage took his thickness between his lips and tugged on Adam's liquefied balls, the mirror captured his attention.

Yes, beyond his reflection in the grimy glass and the ink that had jumped off his arm muscles and into orbit…something other, *more*, attempted to take shape.

"Do you see it?" the Mage asked between gentle sucks on his balls.

"It?"

"The future."

Adam gazed deeper, past the mirror. Yes, as the flickers of his nearing climax tickled his soles, forcing him to the tops of his toes, he could. Space defense forces, massing for a strike. The secret Mage Council, looking forward and backward and beyond in their attempt to glean the biggest possible picture and best outcome, and the Voron-Kali, cruel oppressors over humanity's small wedge of cosmic real estate.

But the glimpse was brief, blurry. Adam's eyes burned and he realized he'd not only been holding his breath but he'd stopped blinking. To blink, to inhale, was to risk losing the vision. Unable to hold back any longer, Adam gave in. Another image formed, tattooed over the insides of his eyelids in temporary ink.

A symbol, one filled with power. Lines and angles, swirls and circular slashes, there one second and gone the next, Adam gasped as his balls pulled up tightly around the root of his length, and his cock unloaded what felt like a gallon of seed down the other man's throat.

***

"Your scent is magnificent," the Mage said.

The sun had yet to rise over Umbra City on Bailey-Vortiss Four, as though the night thirsted for more dark dreams and despair from its residents. Adam sucked down another breath. Their sex had added several new layers of male scent to that which already existed in his hovel.

"Yeah, magnificent," he said, dismissing the statement with a sigh.

"Like pine from the trees on our Mother's soil, and summer rain. And how your sweat varies from one destination on your physique to another—your toes, your balls, your armpits and neck…how I look forward to knowing you better, in every possible way, on the far side of tomorrow."

The Mage's lips pressed against his. Adam kissed, tasting the dregs of his own nectar and the buttery funk of his feet on the other man's lips. Without warning, the image he'd glimpsed on the insides of his eyelids was back, carried on a surge of giddy emotion he didn't immediately recognize. Only after the Mage was back down there, sucking on his toes, worshipping Adam's big feet with kisses and caresses, did he understand that it was hope.

They moved into a position of sacred geometry and flesh—sixty-nine, an all-male yin and yang.

"This future," Adam said while stroking the Mage's tool, an uncircumcised beaut wreathed in chestnut curls that jutted over two impressive balls. "How does it begin?"

"With you boarding the *Colossus at Rhodes*."

An E.E.M. heavy cruiser?

"Yes," the Mage said, as though reading his mind. "Along with *Acropolis*, *Gigantic*, *Mount Helicon*, and *Zhivago*. They're holding in hyperspace, awaiting your arrival."

Imaginary ice formed over Adam's bare spine, cooling his sweat and threatening to consume his reawakened cock. Not that his hardness had ever completely gone down since his encounter with this strange visitor in the tattoo artist guild's emporium. Five of the space defense fleet's surviving capitol ships, gathered in hyperspace for him? One simple man who forged ink on the least of the Archipelago's colonies? The world swam out of focus before Adam's eyes, dissolving in a plethora of black dots.

"Hold steady and hear me. The year-long Rite of Mourning for the late Voron-Kali emperor, Wrux-Lurn, is soon to end, with his successor, Wrux-Imagi, ascending to their throne. While the old guard that conquered our Mother and her colonies maintain solemnity, Imagi has devoted his time to sewing numerous wild oats."

Adam masturbated the other man in slow, upward strokes. "They're all insatiable, that's no secret."

"No, but Imagi is one of the most insatiable of those two-cocked horrors ever born, and he's got a thing for attractive human males."

The Mage glanced up, and Adam didn't need to read minds, tea leaves, or dirty socks to translate the look of desire on the man's face.

"Me?"

"Given all that we know and every forecast made, you are believed to be irresistible to the young emperor's sexual appetite."

Adam jolted in place, tossed back the cover, and hastened out of bed. The hovel, with its single skylight window, trapped him within the tightening press of its walls. He soon found himself back at the mirror, facing his naked reflection. The Mage joined him.

"Imagi will see what I do," the man said. A hand moved over his shoulder and around Adam's chest. "Giving us—the race of man—our one last chance to free our people and planets from their tyranny."

The Mage turned him around. The two men locked eyes in the dim glow. Adam realized that the shadows were withdrawing, the darkness surrendering to day.

"Will you do it?"

Adam shrugged. "Do I have a choice?"

The Mage nodded. Their bodies moved together, male skin on male skin, a silent reminder of all that their race had fought for, and all still left to be battled.

"What do I have to do?" Adam asked.

The Mage tipped his chin and whispered the incantation in Adam's ear. "Tell me about the properties of a certain ink. I believe you call it 'Belgean Clear'."

III.

"Planet Xanadu," the captain of *Colossus at Rhodes* called over the intercom. "Xanadu."

"*Now we are here*," Adam murmured beneath his breath.

Two uniformed soldiers with hard bodies like Luke's and the Mage's escorted him into the landing bay, where rows of beat up Bayonet star fighters were parked, waiting for that suicidal last push should he fail in his mission. Among the Bayonets was a lone stealth transport, a Frankenstein contraption cobbled together by the Mage Council that was constructed of both Earth-based and Voron-Kali tech that had gotten him from the surface of Bailey-Vortiss Four to his rendezvous with his personal guard: five heavy cruisers, flying in staggered wing formation in hyperspace. That's how valuable he was to the E.E.M. cause. And, he suspected, to the Mage.

"Good luck," one of the uniforms said, and saluted.

The other soldier urged him to plunge a sharp object between Imagi's throat and upper chest plates at the first chance possible. "That's where they're most vulnerable, you know. Unless his crotch-shells are open!"

Adam nodded and laughed, though he knew differently. This particular Voron-Kali potentate was most vulnerable in the part of his brain that ruled his two cocks, and besting him there would do Adam's fellow men and women far better in the long term than a blade to the new emperor's throat.

He entered the stealth vehicle and hastily donned the necessary equipment—helmet, atmosphere regulator, communications display all plugging neatly into his flight suit.

"Agent Valico," the captain said.

"Roger, Bridge."

"You know the risk I'm putting my crew and the rest of those patriotic ships in by being here."

Risk? Yes, Adam got it. Intimately. "Yes, sir," he settled for instead.

"You'll have exactly two seconds to vacate the *Colossus's* hangar. Not three. Three means we've just jumped back into hyperspace behind Xanadu's largest moon, and you've been reduced to a million puzzle pieces in the cosmic wind."

Adam checked the display. The stealth vessel's countdown clock was synced-up to that on the bridge of *Colossus at Rhodes*. "Two seconds, understood."

Beyond the direct vision port, Adam saw the *Colossus's* hangar doors roll open. The awesome glare of hyperspace illuminated its proud, sad Bayonet fleet whose pilots lived constantly on the run, were constantly itchy to launch, to fight, to die. The colors attempted to hypnotize him. If he could translate their otherworldly beauty into ink...

"That said, good luck, citizen."

Adam focused. Behind Xanadu's cratered moon Merlin, the *Colossus at Rhodes* flashed out of hyperspace. By that point, Adam had already sent the stealth vessel racing down the launch channel toward the heavy cruiser's open maw. One second later, Adam emerged and activated the ship's anti-detection defenses, which had served him once during his ascent from B-V Four. Two seconds in, the *Colossus at Rhodes* raged back into hyperspace and out of sight, one second before the Voron-Kali satellites in orbit around the planet would have detected her and raised the alarm.

His escort would be deemed just another sensor ghost, Adam thought as he guided the stealth vessel around the moon and toward its destination. At the height of the E.E.M.'s expansion outward from Mother and Sol, Planet Xanadu had been the jewel of colonies. Adam very much doubted that was the case now. The heads-up display noted two-dozen Voron-Kali spine ships in orbit. That number supported the Mage's claim about the timeliness of Adam's arrival, and the presence of Imagi on the surface.

"The corner of Mulberry Street and Anathema Avenue," the man's voice repeated in his thoughts, louder than the broadcasts between enemy capitol ships playing over the radio. So loud, so clear, that Adam looked around, convinced the Mage was in the stealth vessel with him.

But no, a gulf of light-years and vast planetary systems separated them.

He guided the hybrid vessel down through the gap between spine ship formations, clearing the enemy armada as he'd been promised the ship capable of achieving. Down, into Xanadu's atmosphere.

What the Mage hadn't predicted was the high-intensity storm system moving over Coleridge City.

The stealth vessel trembled. The controls bucked. One direct hit from a lightning bolt and he wouldn't be so invisible to prying eyes. Worse, he'd be plummeting out of the sky in chunks.

Adam's heart threw itself against his ribcage and attempted to jump into his throat. The vessel was falling; he was sure of it. He wasn't a pilot, not like those brave, suicidal Bayonet jockeys aboard the *Colossus at Rhodes*. No, he was an ink master skilled at transforming temporary skin into works of art to last a lifetime.

Vertigo attempted to paralyze him. His stomach lurched as up and down switched places. Then he remembered the Mage's handsome face, what the man had done to his body, what he'd said about the future. *Their* future, which was also symbolic of the greater history of mankind.

He righted the vessel and dropped out of the cloud cover. The ground came rushing up. Adam decelerated, vectored toward Coleridge City, and touched down in a vacant stretch of scrubby hardpan within a kilometer of his target. It wasn't the prettiest landing or exactly by the book, but he walked away from it, which made it spectacular.

***

Adam changed into smart socks, a fresh tank, shorts, and new sneakers. It was the perfect ensemble to stoke the young emperor's lust, the Mage had said.

"He'll never be able to resist those incredible legs," the man had added. To drive home the point, the Mage had licked him from furry ankles to shins, dipping behind calves, up past knees to thighs, ending at his balls.

Donning sunglasses, Adam jogged away from the stealth vessel, which had lost a measure of its ability to blend in with its surroundings on impact. The air was warm and smelled of rain and ozone. As he trotted toward the spires of the Ziangdou Towers, his reference point, he again daydreamed of the Mage. If his mission succeeded—if Adam survived—they planned to meet back on Bailey-Vortiss Four. That rendezvous was so far away, it held no more substance than the air he breathed or the hollow plunking melody of the raindrops striking the desiccated ground.

Coleridge City showed time's erosion and Voron-Kali neglect beyond the lenses of his glasses in the abandoned buildings and skeletons of skyscrapers started but never completed. Adam activated the positioning app and the screen inside the lenses directed him right, then left, and left again. Anathema Avenue appeared, one of the city's main thoroughfares. People moved about in spite of the weather. Men, he saw. All were moderately attractive—street trade, as he'd been instructed to expect.

Adam caught several disapproving stares from the competition, which was fine. His destination lay elsewhere.

He continued down Anathema, his heart racing as the corner to Mulberry Street appeared. All of the buildings were made of the sandstone-colored rock quarried from the surrounding landscape, where mountains had been reduced to plains. Adam moseyed to the street corner, knelt down, and retied his sneakers. According to the tiny clock on the inside of his glasses, he was early.

"Help you, pal?" a man's voice asked.

Adam glanced up. Looming over him were two of what he guessed were locals high up on the Coleridge City male escort food chain. They were sex-worthy, he supposed, though their handsomeness was cold, in its last stage of vibrancy, Adam thought. A couple of Coleridge male sex workers who, like flowers already plucked, were poised to fade. Besides, no other man compared to the Mage.

"Gentlemen," Adam said.

He started to stand. The one with the mustache who'd initially addressed him shoved him back down.

"Well, okay," Adam said.

"This is our intersection," the other fading flower said.

Smiling, Adam said, "Then you must be Mister Mulberry, and you, Mister Anathema. A pleasure to meet you!"

He extended his hand and rose to his feet. The first punch nailed Adam's cheek and sent his glasses flying off his face. The second struck the meat of his gut. A galaxy of stars erupted before Adam's eyes and instantly went supernova. By the time the exploding constellations had burned down and Adam could breathe again, they'd dragged him to the steps of one of the nearby buildings.

"Not that I haven't enjoyed your little welcome wagon," he said lightly and chuckled, tasting blood.

Adam shook free, fired a jab, and knocked Mustache off balance. Mister Mulberry made a fist.

Adam danced his right foot between Mulberry's two and tripped him, the formerly conquered conquering his opponents in two swift moves.

"If you want more of me," Adam started. "Come and get it!"

Applause sounded at his back, from the direction of the street. A chill sliced through the heat that enveloped Adam. He instantly sensed the praise hadn't originated from human hands. Turning, he saw the Voron-Kali juggernaut parked at the corner of Mulberry and Anathema, all but its open hatch shimmering with the same near-invisibility as the stealth vessel abandoned at the city's outskirts. Four armed Voron-Kali soldiers stood on the street. An equal number of their snipe fighters hovered over the intersection.

The one applauding was a full foot taller than Adam and dressed in fine raiments that glowed under the moody palette of stormy sky. Adam's next breath hitched halfway up his throat.

"Your Highness," he gasped, and dropped to his knees on the wet sidewalk.

IV.

There were five other men in the juggernaut's private coach. Still bleeding from Mister Anathema's sucker punch, Adam piled in.

"Send the others away, Regent," the emperor commanded. "See that they're all compensated."

The men grumbled, though not too loudly, and exited the coach at the Voron-Kali regent's order. The exodus stirred a pungent mélange of sweat and cologne.

"Please," the emperor said, indicating for Adam to sit. "You are my guest."

"Very kind, Eminence," Adam said.

The emperor sat beside him, and Adam risked his first clear look at the alien potentate close up. He'd seen plenty of Voron-Kali before. Wrux-Imagi was more or less like those others: seven feet tall in height, his skin not quite exoskeletal in design but harder than human epidermis and colored a rosy red, eyes that were all bronze pupil, his body hairless. The two folds of the emperor's pelvic crest were joined to protect Imagi's dual cocks. Four-toed, the emperor wore their version of sandals in addition to the loose-fit robe glowing with numerous colors that teased the ink artist's imagination.

"Not kind at all," Imagi said. "Do you require a doctor?"

Adam flexed his jaw. "No, Majesty—but thank you."

Imagi studied him. "I saw what was done to you on the street, and how you reacted. Impressive. Are you one of the brave former soldiers of the E.E.M.?"

"No, a simple artist."

"An artist? You have me even more intrigued. I noticed the art that decorates your body. May I?"

Adam saw that the new emperor's eyes were aimed at his sleeve of lone star and planets. "You're the Voron-Kali emperor. You don't have to ask."

Imagi's smile widened. "I ask out of respect and admiration."

"Then I give you permission, Highness."

Imagi's smile dropped. The emperor's fingers

caressed Adam's bare arm. "Magnificent."

Fingers wandered from Sol, past humanity's Mother, to Planet Xanadu. Then Wrux-Imagi's other hand settled on Adam's closest leg, stroking muscle before moving higher. From the cut of his wide eyes, Adam saw the emperor's pelvic crest unhinge and relax. Two of the largest cocks he'd ever seen now jutted straight up through the part in Imagi's robes.

"I find you more attractive than any of the males of your species that I've previously had the pleasure of meeting."

"I'm honored, Emperor."

Imagi cupped Adam's cheek and leaned in, stealing a brief kiss that stirred the scent of the alien's flesh, a mix of honey and desert breezes. "I am impressed with your tone of respect—and aroused by your physical perfection. And, I confess, I envy the beauty of the artistry applied to your flesh."

V.

The Ziangdou Towers had once ranked among the E.E.M.'s most luxurious destinations, like the Dardanelles on Landau's World, most of Bailey-Vortiss Two, and the Alpine resorts on Mother Earth.

While humans no longer occupied the Towers, their former elegance had been maintained for the Voron-Kali. The emperor's accommodations were housed on the top floor of Olympus Tower, with stunning views of the city, spaceport, and the surrounding desert.

After Imagi's private physician deemed Adam clear of all communicable diseases—passion-centered as well as other afflictions able to be transmitted between humans and Voron-Kali—and had determined he wasn't carrying micro-firearms or harboring any subcutaneous or blood-based weaponry, Imagi ordered all retinue out of his chambers.

"Many human males, here and on other colonies, have been invited into my bed," Imagi said. The emperor licked his lips. "None have stoked my arousal so completely, Adam the Artist."

Imagi dropped his robes. Both of the emperor's cocks stood at their stiffest condition. The counterfeit smile on Adam's face, at first, felt like betrayal to both the Mage and to his race as a whole. Then, removing his tank top, Adam remembered that everything that was to follow was done in service to and out of love for them.

***

As their time together deepened, Adam sensed Imagi's sincerity on certain matters, such as the roles they soon took to after their first time together in the emperor's bed. Imagi was ravenous for Adam's cock, and the majority of their sex was oral, with the young emperor greedily swallowing down the artist's nectar and seeing that he was well fed on a sumptuous diet that supported male human sexual health. In addition to Imagi's tongue wandering Adam's physique, the Voron-Kali emperor renounced much of his power through willing submission, allowing Adam to dominate him, which led to Imagi brooding from embarrassment post-coitus.

"What is wrong, Emperor?" Adam asked.

He knelt between Imagi's bare legs and gazed up.

Initially, the emperor avoided his eyes. When they connected, Adam saw Imagi's intense longing.

"What can I do?" Adam asked, caressing the emperor's leg.

"You can ease my worry. Tell me this means more to you than only lust or reward, Adam."

Adam boldly reached higher and touched Imagi's cheek. He envisioned the bronze eyes as being gray, wolfish. "From the moment I looked and you were standing there on the street, my artist's eye was seduced, and my heart fell."

"I love you," the emperor confessed. "I love your scent, the way you taste, your legs, your cock, and your ink."

From out of the days past, he heard the voice of the soldier on board the heavy cruiser *Colossus at Rhodes* telling him to stab at Wrux-Imagi's throat at the first opportunity. A wave of sadness attempted to wash over Adam as he stroked the emperor's cheek and Imagi leaned into his touch. He had the enemy leader where he wanted him, only it wasn't the joyous victory he'd anticipated.

Adam cleared his throat. He was about to suggest he tattoo the Voron-Kali emperor when Imagi said, "Ink me, please, Adam, my love…"

VI.

"For my public coronation," Wrux-Imagi said. "In your body art, you have conquered all of human space. As I take to the Grand Proscenium on my home world of Voron-Kal and drop my robes in honor of Leus the

First, let me show the empire new ideas and ways of leading."

Adam's cock thickened, helped along more by the manifestation of the Mage's plan than Imagi's upward jerks. "It would be my honor."

"Yes, it would, *human*," Imagi growled, a rare reasserting of his authority behind closed doors. "No Voron-Kali before me will have looked so regal! And, in return, I will show greater favor to your people and their former planets than my predecessor."

"You are gracious as well as noble," Adam said.

Imagi grinned. "I've never felt this happy or certain. I will rule, and you will be at my side as official human consort. And before I take to the Proscenium for all to see, you will transform me into art."

Adam made a list of requirements—needles and types of ink, sketchbook and pens so he could hand draw the templates for Wrux-Imagi's transformation. Supplies arrived from Coleridge City's finest art houses and, once deemed safe by the regent, Adam began to work.

Across the emperor's chest, he depicted the Mountain of Fog, the most sacred image in Voron-Kali doctrine, where, according to legend, the Pantheon spoke to the prophet Leus the First, imparting their laws to mortals. For days, Imagi admired the results in the mirror and proved in actions as well as words his love for Adam's creation.

Next, Adam worked twin black stars with eight points across the halves of the emperor's pelvic crest. Though the universe was a dangerous realm, often unforgiving, the power contained behind the crest, the might of Voron-Kali cocks, would always prevail.

They made love, and Imagi again professed his devotion to Adam and fairer times for his species beneath Voron-Kali rule.

"Lie on your stomach," Adam instructed.

Imagi stretched across the bed. Naked, Adam straddled the emperor's bare back.

"Are you sure, Highness?"

Imagi nodded. "For the gifts you have given me, I offer this blank canvas in thanks. Create that which you desire."

Adam set the needle against the tough flesh of the emperor's upper shoulder. He would recreate his own sleeve of star and planets, which Imagi had made clear he loved. Adam inked, wiped. The colonial realm of the former E.E.M. took shape across its conqueror's back.

And then, superimposed over the planets, he saw the powerful symbol that had teased him in his hovel back on Bailey-Vortiss Four, angles and circular arcs, forming an image of great significance and power.

As though in a trance, Adam reached for the tube of Belgean Clear ink. He began to draw the precise vision burning brightly in his thoughts.

VII.

"Star and planets," the Voron-Kali emperor said, admiring the reflection of the artwork inked into the flesh of his back. "You've done incredible work."

He gently touched Adam's chin.

"Come, for we must depart for the Voron-Kal home world."

***

Emperor Wrux-Imagi glided onto the Proscenium, his arrival applauded by the two thousand social, political, military, and clerical dignitaries in attendance.

"Do you vow to honor each and every promise signed into law, as Leus kept true to his promise to the Pantheon?"

Imagi nodded. "I swear to uphold every promise I make, in Leus's name."

The regent lowered the crown onto Imagi's head. The new emperor tipped a look toward the right of the throne, where his human consort stood. The emperor smiled, extended his arms, and dropped his robes, in deference to Leus, who'd returned from the Mountain of Fog naked. Those present and watching across Voron-Kali space saw the tattoos of the foggy mountain, the black stars, and, when Imagi turned, the star map inked over his bare back. By then, the Belgean Clear ink had darkened and set, forming the holy symbol of Leus the First, which he'd brought back from his meeting with the Pantheon on the Mountain of Fog. The symbol, translated from the Old Voron-Kali tongue, represented mercy. But also more. A promise of release from bondage.

The applause quieted, replaced by gasps.

"What is wrong?" asked Imagi.

One week later, the abolishment contract with humanity was ratified, and the Voron-Kali war machine began its withdrawal from E.E.M. space.

VIII.

Adam aimed the key at the door. The lock turned. Clearly, even given the joyous atmosphere across their Mother's liberated territories, the desire to live in Umbra on B-V Four still hadn't amounted to a land grab.

The apartment was how he'd left it months earlier, a mess haunted by traces of lovemaking past. He set down his bags, closed the door, and ran water in a glass. The faucet's cold temperature had never gone better than tepid, the taste gritty, and those things were still so now on the other side of his return from the Voron-Kali home world. He drank, appreciating the reliability of his old life's fixtures.

Adam set down the empty glass and wandered over to the mirror. The eye patch was a new addition to the hovel's reflected landscape. He'd also aged spiritually, as well as in the physical sense. For a second, perhaps two, he worried he might cry. One of his tear ducts had survived Imagi's rage intact and stung, but he willed it to hold back the deluge.

A knock sounded at the door. Adam shook himself out of the trance and answered. The Mage stood outside.

"Welcome home, Adam."

Adam embraced the other man and crushed their mouths together. Closing the door, he silently walked the Mage over to the bed, eager to begin the future they'd envisioned.

EMBODY
BY LIVIA VITALI

BELL FELT THE HEAT RISE BETWEEN HER LEGS as she looked up at her Mistress. She hardly noticed the chill in the air of the pinup style tattoo parlor. All it took was one stern and seductive glance of Mistress's dark eyes and she was wet. Squirming in the red vinyl chair, watching her Mistress as she instructed the artist on the style of the tattoo she was to receive on her lower back.

Needles were nothing to mess with in Bell's eyes. She had no interest in a tattoo. But she certainly wanted to please Mistress, and that meant obeying and being branded with Mistress's very own art.

She didn't know what the tattoo would look like. No idea whatsoever. She hoped it wasn't some kind of silly saying like, "owned," or, "slave girl." While those could be fun, Bell didn't think she wanted that permanently branded on her lower back.

She watched as Mistress's long, red hair fell over her should. Then followed the contours of her body down to her breasts, bulging from her white, button up blouse. With the first three buttons undone, as always. Then down to her tight, floor-length skirt hiding the boots she'd made Bell lace up perfectly before leaving the house.

The tattoo artist was a man in his mid-forties. Some speckles of white hair, a finely trimmed beard, and neck to toe tattoos of his own. He wore shorts on a dismal fall day, and a t-shirt that seemed entirely too tight for his thick frame. Bell wondered if he was just that proud of his body art or if he'd grown accustomed to the chilly air.

Likely the first, she thought.

Their voices were low, but still carried across the room. She thought she'd heard Mistress say, "temptress," but that didn't fit her. She must have said something else.

Bell leaned back into the chair and waited. Her thoughts racing as to what Mistress had planned. She loved not knowing, which worked out well for them since Mistress never told Bell of her plans.

She traced the contours of the ceiling tile with her eyes. Making shapes in her mind as she located broken pieces barely gripping their glue. Bell shivered as sudden awareness grabbed hold in her chest. Soon that strange man would be marking her indefinitely and the parlor appeared to be falling apart.

Then again, they were downtown. So many old buildings had been renovated and turned into flourishing businesses. No, she thought, Mistress wouldn't have brought me if there were any danger.

Before she finished her thoughts on it, Mistress and the stranger approached.

"Bell, meet Tempeh. He will be your artist for today."

Bell reached up to shake the man's hand and said, "Nice to meet you, Tempeh."

"Likewise, Bell. Shall we get started?"

Bell nodded.

Tempeh had Bell sign forms and consent to being tattooed without knowledge of what was going on her. Which all seemed reasonable and lifted Bell's fears some. Then he told her to lay on her stomach. Mistress pulled Bell's skirt down and blouse up to reveal the exact location to be branded.

As Tempeh readied his tools, Bell felt her back tense. Mistress must have seen her, because she rubbed Bell's head gently, as if to reassure her.

All Bell could see was the red of the vinyl chair. She'd buried her head well. The fact she'd not safeworded when Mistress wanted to tattoo her had shocked even her. With Bell's extreme fear of needles, this was a huge step.

Mistress leaned down and whispered into Bell's ear. "For being such a good girl, Mistress is going to make you come again and again." Then she kissed Bell's ear and Bell peeked to the side just in time to see her Mistress stand.

Tempeh put something that felt like paper on her back. It was cold and felt wet. She smelled something antibacterial in nature.

Bell squirmed.

"Hold still," Mistress said.

Bell stilled.

She didn't want to watch as the Tempeh readied his tools. She'd seen earlier two distinct colors, but they didn't make sense yet. Plus, she had no way of knowing if both would be used or if more would be added. She'd seen black and red.

After Tempeh and Mistress agreed that the tattoo looked to be in the right location, Tempeh reached for his tool and shifted his foot over a pedal on the floor. Bell sucked in her breath, knowing he was about to start. She tried hard not to move.

The gun hummed like the dentist drill and a flash of pain shot through her before the needle even hit her delicate skin. The moment he made contact, Bell cried out a muffled, "Ouch!" from under her hair and arms. She'd buried herself in her own body for comfort.

Mistress rubbed her head as Bell tried to suppress her tears. It stung, burned, not anything like the dentist drill. This was far worse. And Bell still hated needles.

"You're doing well, girl," Mistress said.

Bell focused on her breath. Keeping each in and out breath timed, just as she did while Mistress beat her. She wanted so badly to be on the cross so she'd drop into subspace and not feel the tattoo, but that couldn't happen.

"Mistress?" Bell barely got her word out under her suppressed tears.

"Yes, girl?"

"Will you drop me a bit please?"

Her tone was one of surrender and desperation. She could hear it even in her own voice. She also knew her Mistress was gracious and would help her.

Mistress grabbed Bell's hair firmly and without yanking her head, then whispered into her ear, "Ten, nine, eight, deep girl…"

Bell felt herself dropping for Mistress. Her body

relaxing as she pictured herself on the cross, Mistress pacing behind her with her cane.

Bell loved the cane.

She felt herself begin to squirm and had to focus to hold steady.

"Good, girl," Mistress said. "You'll have more numbers as Tempeh gets further into the tattoo."

Bell whimpered under Mistress's hand. She wanted more numbers now, but suspected Mistress didn't want her too deep yet. Not with so much time still ahead. So Bell let her mind wander instead. She thought of all the lovely things Mistress did to her last night. How she'd made Bell bathe her, then pulled Bell into the tub as well, fully clothed.

How she'd forced Bell's head under the water to eat her Mistress. Bell loved it when Mistress did things like that. Just thinking about it made her cunt moist. She remembered running her tongue along Mistress's clit as she held her breath. Feeling the sting in her lungs while she pleasured Mistress.

The sting on her back only made the memory stronger.

Later Mistress had made Bell crawl to bed. She had to kneel at Mistress's feet and beg to join her in bed. She'd begged well, and Mistress had pulled out Bell's collar from her nightstand drawer.

Bell felt the collar around her neck as she imagined this happening now. The hum of the tattoo tool suddenly helpful in keeping her in a state of comfort and bliss; the burn a reminder of Mistress's painful lessons.

The imaginary collar felt heavy and thick around

her neck. She shifted slightly as if Mistress had put it on this morning.

"What are you doing, girl?" Mistress asked.

"Feeling your collar, Mistress," Bell barely got her words out.

"Good, girl."

Tempeh kept stopping, and Bell didn't want to look. Mistress had already warned her not to before they'd arrived. She assumed he was doing something with ink, or maybe he was readjusting. She didn't know.

She focused on her imaginary collar again. Letting all her focus shift there as he touched the needle to her skin again and the burn came right back. Each time he moved over the dip in her lower back, a deeper pain shot through her.

Bell whimpered again.

"Seven, six, five," Mistress said.

Bell felt her eyes roll as Mistress's words carried deep within her.

"Thank you, Mistress."

When Mistress reached zero, Bell knew she got to come like a little whore for her. She also knew Mistress wouldn't let her do it until they were done, lest she desired to have a random tattoo line running across her back.

The numbers carried her deeper though, and Bell's senses heightened. The pain in her back began to feel like pleasure.

This was what Bell had hoped for.

She gasped, but this time with a hint of pleasure.

Mistress must have heard her, because she laughed,

then rubbed her head again.

Each new line felt like Mistress's cane. The sting and following pain made her wetter. The muscles inside her cunt tightened with each tiny movement of the gun. It took all of her focus not to sway her hips back and forth on the vinyl chair. She wanted to desperately.

The deeper Bell fell into subspace, the more she heard Mistress's breath and nothing else. Even the hum of the tattoo tool faded. Bell breathed all the way to her cunt. Feeling each breath like the hint of orgasm.

Mistress continued to run her hand across Bell's hair, and she wanted so badly to nuzzle up to her like a feline desiring to be pet. An unfamiliar fire began to grow in Bell. One she didn't understand and had never felt before.

Her heart raced at the feeling.

"Mistress?"

"Yes, girl?"

"There's something wrong. I'm burning inside. It feels funny."

"Like what, girl?"

"It feels like this weird fire. When I breathe in, it travels all the way down. Then back up when I breathe out. It hurts, Mistress."

"You love pain, don't you, slut?" Mistress's words went in like the fire too, straight down and in between Bell's legs. She felt the pain and fire as pleasure.

As ecstasy.

"Yes, Mistress," her words came out like pleasure too. "What's happening to me?"

"Tempeh is finishing up with the outline."

"Okay, Mistress. But what's happening to me? I

don't understand this fire. Or this painful pleasure."

"Tempeh is finishing up with the outline," she repeated.

Bell squinted her hidden eyes. What on earth did Mistress mean? How did Tempeh finishing the outline have anything to do with this bizarre feeling inside her?

Bell breathed deeply. Sucking in all the breath she could just as Tempeh removed the needle again. This time he set it down on the metal table. Bell knew from the sound of metal on metal, though she wasn't watching. Her face was still hidden beneath her hair and arms.

Mistress shifted positions and whispered into Bell's ear, "You may come until I tell you to stop."

Bell's inner muscles flexed and tightened as she prepared for Mistress to say zero, but something unexpected happened. Instead, Mistress left Bell's head area and leaned over her lower back. She breathed gently across where the fresh tattoo outline lay.

The moment Mistress's breath hit the tattoo, fire tore through her. Orgasmic fire. She came up off the chair as the orgasm rushed through her body like a flash flame. She clenched the vinyl chair and cried out, "Thank you, Mistress!"

Each breath Mistress blew on her caused a new orgasm. Bell's head spun. She couldn't understand. She knew counting down made her come, but that was many months of training. Not an easy thing. This was different. Unexpected.

Tempeh laughed in a deep voice, "I didn't think that would have the effect you were hoping for." His words seemed directed to Mistress. "I was wrong."

Mistress laughed, and stopped breathing on her back.

"I know what I'm doing," she told him.

"I'm ready to begin filling it in now," Tempeh said.

"Noted." Mistress moved back up to Bell's head, caressed her again, and whispered into her ear, "There's more to come, but for now, you must be still again. No more orgasms."

"Yes, Mistress." Bell forced her body to calm down. It wasn't easy. She'd never come like that before.

The moment Tempeh's tool hummed again and made contact with her skin, the scent of sandalwood and jasmine filled her senses. Overwhelming her completely.

The scents brought a sense of stillness and peace.

"What is that you're putting on me?" she asked Tempeh.

"I don't know what you mean. The ink? I'm not supposed to tell you the color," he said with a hint of confusion in his tone.

"She doesn't mean that," Mistress interjected.

"It's the sandalwood and jasmine. It smells so good," Bell said.

"The what?" Tempeh laughed his words.

"Sandalwood and jasmine," Bell repeated.

"I…" Tempeh began, but Mistress interrupted again.

"He's not putting that on you, girl. You are the only one who smells it."

His gun moved over her skin causing more pain than the outline. But this time Bell's endorphins kept her from wanting to jump.

"I don't understand. How can I smell these things?"

"You'll know soon enough, girl." Mistress ran her hand through Bell's hair.

Bell felt like purring under her hand again. She allowed herself to check out and enjoy the smells and fire once more. Holding as still as possible as she did so.

Hours passed, she was certain. She wanted so badly to move. Her muscles were tired and sore and she needed to pee desperately. Bell was just about to ask for a break when Tempeh's tool stopped and he set it down a final time.

"Done," he said.

Bell looked up to see both Tempeh and Mistress standing to inspect his work.

"This looks amazing, Tempeh. You are a master of the art of tattooing," Mistress said.

"Thank you. Let me get her cleaned up and we'll take care of payment," he said.

Mistress leaned down before Bell and looked her in the eyes. "I'm proud of you, girl."

"Thank you, Mistress. Can I see it now?"

"Not yet, girl."

Bell's heart felt like it dropped to her feet as she looked up at Mistress. She felt her lips purse into a pout.

"You'll see soon enough, girl." Mistress patted her head, and walked away with Tempeh.

Bell waited patiently for Tempeh to finish up and cover her new masterpiece so she could finally pee. When she was done, she stood to find that there were several colors on the metal table. Blue, orange, yellow, and brown had been added. Bell didn't remember that many changes of ink, but then again, she had been pretty out of it.

"Where's the restroom?" Bell asked.

Tempeh pointed to the front of the building. Mistress followed Bell in.

"Have I done something wrong, Mistress?"

"No, girl. I don't want you peeking." She smiled.

Mistress watched her as she peed. It was lovely and humiliating. Bell felt her heart beat faster as she thought of what was now permanently on her back.

They finished up at the tattoo parlor, thanked Tempeh, and left.

As they walked to the car, Bell began to fidget.

"Mistress, when do I get to see? I really want to know what's on my back."

"You'll know tonight. You won't need to see to figure it out." Mistress laughed, sending Bell into a deeper state of consciousness again. "Now get in the car and relax. You'll know soon enough."

Bell obeyed, and was careful not to press up against her new marking. It was tender, and the seat felt hard. She focused on the fire she'd felt earlier, and buckled up.

***

Bell walked behind Mistress past the cross, the spanking bench, the suspension hooks, and her favorite—the suspension bar. She loved holding the bar, hanging from it as Mistress took the cane to her. Others were playing at the stations, though stopped as Bell passed them.

Bell's collar was tight around her neck, leash

sparkling in the dungeon light. Mistress had her wear her black dress that cut so low the top of her butt showed. It was her favorite. Perfect for showing off her new artwork.

The silky fabric brought comfort to her as her fellow kinky friends watched her walk behind Mistress. Bell puffed her chest out, proud to be the submissive little slut she was. No matter what they stared at on her back.

Bell felt sexy. Beautiful. Graceful behind Mistress.

She watched as Mistress's hips swayed, feeling it all the way to her cunt as she got wet for Mistress. Which only made Bell's hips sway more, her walk like a dance of sex as she thought of pleasing Mistress.

Mistress laughed, and Bell looked around to see why. She didn't understand what she was seeing, because no one was looking at Mistress. They were looking at her.

She felt heat rush her cheeks and she stopped walking.

People looked strange. Her friends were squirming as they watched her. Bell grimaced.

Her Mistress turned around and caressed Bell's cheek. "Relax, girl. You are powerful. Be yourself."

"But, Mistress, I'm your sub. How am I powerful? I don't understand why everyone is looking at me."

Tears welled in her eyes, and Mistress leaned into Bell.

"Open your mouth, girl."

Bell obeyed.

Mistress breathed into her mouth, and Bell felt it all the way to her cunt. It made her come hard, right there in front of everyone, with nothing more than breath.

And as she did, the tattoo on her back felt like fire again. Which only made her come harder.

She moaned, and Mistress held her up as she tried to fall to her knees. Mistress leaned down whispered into her ear, "Lust."

Bell's knees buckled and she fell, despite her Mistress's attempts.

Her Mistress leaned down to whisper another word, "Desire."

Then love.

Passion.

Sexual pleasure.

The words ran deep into Bell, and she kept coming. It wasn't stopping. One long orgasm. The harder she came, the lower to the ground she moved. Her hips moved back and forth as she felt something in her rising. From the same fire rose a serpent of energy. Snaking its way up her body and out of her mouth.

Before she could comprehend, her friends were gathering around her. She looked up to see their eyes in a trance like state. Their mouths slightly open. Pupils dilated. She was somehow feeding their state with her own.

Mistress kept repeating the same words and Bell began to smell jasmine and sandalwood once again. Her mind drifted and visions of her dancing in fire entered her mind. Swirling and swaying, her hips still moving. The more she saw it in her mind, the more she acted this very scene out.

Before she'd realized it, Mistress had removed her leash and Bell was dancing around the room. A dungeon full of play areas and everyone was still watching her.

Following her.

Breathing deeply as if they were hypnotized by her movements.

Bell felt heaviness on her chest, and she danced toward Mistress. Panic obvious in her eyes. She grabbed on to Mistress, who embraced her with a firm grasp.

"Be who you are, my little goddess."

Mistress's words once again carried through her, reaching all the way to her cunt. She looked into Mistress's eyes, deep into them. She felt her power. The power Mistress had said she had, but she couldn't feel it prior. This was what she'd meant.

Bell was a Goddess.

This was what Mistress had tattooed on her. She knew it. Felt it.

Bell stopped fighting the feeling building inside her. She surrendered to it. With one exception…

"Mistress? I don't want to be powerful if I can't submit to you."

"Ah, but my little goddess, the more power you possess, the more you can give to me when you submit. I want you powerful. I want you to be you." Mistress smiled, her eyes gentle yet full of their own power. The power Bell had come to love.

"I love you, Mistress."

"I love you too, little goddess. Now… Be you. Be powerful. Dance your goddess dance."

Bell let go and felt music moving through her. A strange beat that wasn't actually in the room. If felt like a beat of earth. Life. Rising up from beneath her and moving through her. Influencing her movements.

She danced around the room, occasionally touching people, and they'd fall to their knees. Bell felt high as she allowed Goddess to move through her. To use her body as a vessel. All the while watching her beautiful Mistress from across the room.

Mistress had changed into her dark purple corset with matching skirt before they'd left home. Her red hair was pulled up, exposing her petite neck. She was letting Bell's leash dangle from her fingers. It still sparkled under the dim dungeon lighting.

Bell smiled herself this time, and let her hips move in a dance of desire toward Mistress. Others danced with her, and some regained their composure as Bell focused her energy toward Mistress instead.

Mistress stood taller. Her breasts pushed outward and toward Bell. Which only made Bell wetter.

Bell fell to her knees and crawled to Mistress. The fire in her back made its way to her cunt, then up to her heart, throat, mouth, and it continued until she felt ablaze as she reached Mistress's feet.

She leaned down and kissed Mistress's feet.

Mistress grabbed her by the hair and pulled hard, giving Bell that lovely feeling of submission. Mistress met Bell's eyes, and began counting again. Picking up where she'd left off at the tattoo parlor.

"Five, four, three," Mistress's voice grew deeper with each lowered number.

Bell squirmed, the fire in her building as the tingles rushed between her legs.

"You've been a good girl today, little goddess. Mistress is pleased."

Bell squirmed more.

"Would my girl like to come again?"

"Yes, please, Mistress."

Bell closed her eyes and let Mistress's energy mix with her own. She let the Goddess fill her too. Her swaying hips and the feeling of her kundalini were far more intense than any submission she'd ever felt.

"Two... one..." Mistress was dragging it out, her numbers louder and more forceful as the counted down.

It felt like several minutes passed and Bell began to feel desperation kick in.

"Please let me come, Mistress? Please, Mistress?" Bell pleaded.

Mistress lifted her skirt and right leg, resting it on a stool next to her. She smelled Mistress's sweet scent, and it made her beg more. Mistress had no panties on.

"Please, Mistress! Please let me lick your cunt and come for you! Please?"

Mistress pulled Bell by the hair and shoved her face into her wet pussy. Bell felt the fire move to her tongue as she buried her face in Mistress. Lapping up every juice and running her tongue along Mistress's clit.

"Use your fingers too, my little goddess."

Bell shoved two fingers inside Mistress. She felt her ready to come. Mistress's muscles moving and clenching, gripping her fingers tightly as she neared orgasm.

Bell's own muscles clenched as well. Feeling her Mistress about to come was overwhelming, and Bell could hardly hold on. Mistress's pussy was so warm and inviting.

Just when Bell didn't think she could hold off any longer, she heard the words she'd been pleading for.

"Zero! Come for Mistress, goddess!"

Bell cried out into Mistress's pussy as she came hard. Her cries made Mistress's inner muscles clench around her fingers as Mistress came too. Both letting out noises of pleasure as they released for all to see.

The fire felt like it moved from Bell and into Mistress. She couldn't be certain, but it felt that way. Then it would come back to her like a feedback loop of fire and orgasm.

Of pure pleasure.

Bell collapsed at Mistress's feet. Her body spent as she finished coming on the ground. Everything went quiet within her, and it was only then that Mistress pulled her to her feet and faced her toward everyone watching.

To Bell's surprise, everyone that had gone back to playing had once again stopped. All eyes on her.

"You see who you are now, my little goddess? Do you know what is on your back?"

"A Goddess, Mistress?"

"Any particular?"

Bell thought hard and remembered her book on Hindu Goddesses. Mistress had gotten it for her sometime back. The memory was faint, but she'd read the words Mistress had said to her earlier. Lust, sexual desire, passion, love…

She dug deep in her thoughts to locate the Goddess's name, and finally, it came to her.

"Rati, Mistress," she paused as the rest sank in. "That's who is on my back."

"Good little goddess. Mistress is proud of you."

Bell smiled all the way to her cunt. She didn't need to see the tattoo, though she'd look anyway first chance she got. Bell knew who she was. Who was on her back…

Bell was powerful.

She embodied Rati.

COMMITMENT
BY KATYA HARRIS

"ARE YOU READY?"

I lick my lips and try to smother the butterflies trying to beat their way out of my belly. "Yes. I'm ready."

Andre smiles and it's worth everything to see that familiar crooked grin, the approval glimmering in his dark eyes. He's excited. If I look at his groin, I know he'll be deliciously full and hard behind his tight black jeans. His smile widens, knowing that I know how he feels. Without looking away from my face, he says, "Okay, Patrick. Let's get started."

Sitting next to me on a little wheeled stool, Patrick chuckles. My eyes leap to his, colliding with his baby blues. I don't know him, have never met him before, but I know he is excited too. It's there in the flush of his cheeks, his hot eyes, and reddened lips.

My breaths quicken. My pussy heats up. Beneath the tank top I'm wearing, my nipples harden to aching points. I'm not wearing a bra—Andre told me not to— and the stiff tips press against the thin, silky fabric. Patrick's gaze dips down and the blue of his eyes intensify to the colour of a flame's heart. His hand tightens around the machine he's holding, his gloves stretching tight over his knuckles. I've been trying to ignore the black latex gloves he's wearing—the sight of them, the thought of them on my skin, does funny things to me.

"Okay," Patrick says. With his other hand, he hitches up the leg of his worn black jeans. "Let's get this show on the road."

They have already prepared me. Andre tied and pinned my long hair to the top of my head, making sure not a single strand hung down to get in the way. Then Patrick painstakingly stencilled the design onto me, and now it's time for him to put the needle to my skin.

Dread and excitement swirl together in my belly. The sudden buzz of the tattoo gun as Patrick switches it on, makes me jump. The tattoo parlour is empty except for us and the noise pops the bubble of quiet that surrounds us. I whimper, every muscle in my body tightening. My mouth floods with the coppery taste of adrenaline.

"Easy, darling. Just look at me."

Andre's voice soothes me. I look at him, let him see the fear and anticipation in my eyes, and watch as he drinks it in. When Patrick's needle touches my skin, I gasp. Pain flares, more intense than I'd thought it would be, and I let Andre see that too.

The needle traces over my skin, following the path Patrick lay so carefully with his stencil. I try to breath slowly, smoothly, but every now and again the pain crescendos, and I hiss. Sometimes, Patrick stops and uses a paper towel to wipe away the excess ink—the sand-papery texture rasping over my freshly pierced and coloured skin, is another kind of hurt.

I steel myself and endure, and never once do I look away from Andre's face.

I don't know how long it's been when the buzz of the tattoo gun stops.

"How are you doing?"

The stare I've been sharing with Andre stretches like toffee before I can break it. I blink at Patrick. "I'm okay." My voice is slurred; I sound the way I do when I'm in sub-space. I am there a little bit I realise, the warm familiar sea lapping at my fingers and toes.

Turning his head, Patrick shares a grin with Andre. "I think she likes it."

I want to say I'm not sure of that, but all I can seem to do is smile dreamily. Perhaps he's right after all.

"Let's see, shall we." Andre touches the pad of his index finger to my chin, turning my head to look back at him. "Lift up your skirt, darling."

I whimper, my cheeks burning red, but my hands are already moving. The skirt I'm wearing is short and loose; gathering up the material in both hands, I lift it to expose my pussy. It's naked, both of panties and hair, the lips smooth and utterly exposed between my pressed together thighs.

"Open your legs."

I do, spreading them wide and letting my lower legs dangle over the sides of the tattoo chair. The cool air of the tattoo parlour kisses my pussy and I shiver. Well, it could be that or the way that the two men in front of me are looking at my cunt, like there's treasure between my legs. I'm already wet, but the looks on their faces make me even wetter.

"You're right, Patrick," Andre says, "I think she does like it."

"Then we should carry on." Patrick's voice is deeper than before, lustful. There's an edge of anticipation to it and for the first time, I wonder what else Andre has planned for the night.

The buzz of the tattoo gun fills the space. It kisses my skin, a thousand bites and stings, and my legs tighten around the chair. My hands hold on tight to the fabric of my skirt. I bite my lip. My clit throbs, wanting to be touched. My pussy aches, wanting to be filled.

Pain moves through me, every nerve in my body resonating in sympathy. I want to squirm, to writhe, to bear down with my hips and grind my cunt against the leather beneath me. That I can't, that I have to hold perfectly still, makes the urge all the worse. My breaths shudder in and out of my lungs. My lips part and my eyes widen.

Patrick moves around me. He's so close I can feel his hot breaths against my skin, smell the spicy musk of his aftershave, brasher than Andre's scent. He smells good and he feels good too. My skin pebbles with goose bumps whenever he touches me with his strong hands in their rubbery latex gloves. He feels sinister and it's darkly exciting.

My fingers twitch, almost brushing against the mound of my sex.

"Ah-ah-ahh," Andre admonishes.

I whimper, a pleading little mewl.

"Be patient," he croons. "You'll be done soon. Right, Patrick?"

"Almost done," Patrick tells him. He's circled me and is almost back to where he started.

"I can't," I whisper. I draw in a shuddering breath. "I can't bear it."

Andre's face doesn't change, but his eyes sparkle with laughter. "Oh, my poor darling." Moving closer, he reaches down between my legs. His blunt fingers slide boldly between the slick folds of my cunt. "So wet." A bland observation, like he's talking about the weather. He circles the hard bud of my clit then burrows down to pierce my pussy with two hard fingers.

I was wrong. I can't bear this. I moan, low and feral, my core shaking with the warring needs to move and keep still. If I ruin the tattoo, Andre will be so cross, I remind myself.

Reading me in that way of his, he says, "Don't move. Keep still."

I cling to his commands.

"You're not helping my concentration," Patrick complains. "But you're lucky because we—are—done."

The buzzing stops at the same moment that Andre slips his fingers from me. Patrick rubs the paper towel against my skin for hopefully the last time, and the pain goes from an immediate agony to a sharp throb.

"There. Finished." Pushing his stool back a little, he looks at my face. "Do you want to see?" Patrick asks me.

"Yes."

He holds up a mirror and I stare at my reflection, entranced.

Delicate curls and swirls circle my throat, stretching from my jaw to collarbone. It looks like the finest lace has been bound around my neck, the pure, virginal white of it brilliant against my reddened skin.

"It will be more subtle when it heals up," Patrick tells me. Reaching out he brushes a gloved finger just below the edge of the tattoo at the hollow of my throat. When he speaks, his voice is softer, warmer. "It will look gorgeous against your golden skin."

I blush. My head is already spinning from all the endorphins and adrenaline surging through me—the pleasure of his caress, his words, is more than I can bear.

I lean into his touch. My skin is buzzing almost as harshly as his tattoo gun had done, desperate for more.

Flattening his hand on the top of my chest, Patrick strokes his thumb over the dip between my collarbones.

"What do you think, Andre?" Patrick asks. "Did I do a good job?"

My husband moves closer, comes to stand beside Patrick. "I think you did beautifully." His eyes glitter with a possessive gleam. "Do you like it, darling?"

Not looking away from the reflection of Patrick's hand on me, I say, "I love it."

That's a lie. Love is too weak a word for what I feel. This is the permanent mark of our commitment, not just of our marriage, but our Dominant and submissive relationship. This is a collar I will never be able to take off, and I adore it.

"Good." Patrick smiles. "Let me just put some gel on it."

Picking up a new tube from his workstation, Patrick squeezes some of the gel onto his fingers and gently spreads a thick layer over my neck, covering my new tattoo completely. I sigh, appreciating the coolness on my inflamed skin.

"There. That should help with the pain. I'll give you a couple of tubes and a pamphlet about how to care for the tattoo before you go."

"I'll take care of her too," Andre tells him. "Don't worry." Beneath his handmade suits, Andre's body is decorated with many works of art, most done by Patrick himself.

Patrick grins at him. "I know you do, man, but it's habit." Patrick pulls off his gloves, the snap of the latex loud. I can't stop a flash of disappointment.

"I think my wife likes your gloves."

I should have known Andre wouldn't miss that.

One of Patrick's eyebrows, the one pierced with two gleaming silver rings, quirks upward in a sharp arch. "Oh really?" His grin pulls at the corner of his mouth. He has really nice lips, full and firm looking, the bottom one a little plumper in the middle—it just begs to be sucked on.

"Well," Patrick continues, "I have plenty more pairs."

My breath hitches, betraying me.

Andre smiles at me, but speaks to Patrick. "Put some on."

As we'd gotten ready this evening I had caught a glimpse of a familiar dark look on Andre's face, and I'd known he'd been planning something. So I'm not exactly surprised when he says, "stand up."

His voice has become deeper, inflexible: his Dom voice. It makes every cell in my body stand to attention.

Patrick pushes with his feet against the floor, moving his little stool back just enough to give me some space to do as I am told. I stand up. My skirt brushes against my thighs as it falls back down. My palms are sweaty so I wipe them against the front of my skirt.

Stepping in front of me, Andre holds my eyes with his as he put his hands on my hips. They are hot through the thin material of my clothes.

"We have to be very, very careful of your new tattoo so you're going to have be good and hold still. Do you understand?"

I swallow and the movement of my throat makes the pain flare. It bands my neck, like a hand with a slightly too-tight grip. Like Andre's hand.

"I understand, Sir."

He smiles and it's like the sunrise, warm with his approval. "Good girl."

His fingers find the zipper of my skirt and pull it down. My skirt falls to the floor, puddling around my feet. Andre's hands go to the hem of my tank top next, carefully lifting it up. I raise my arms automatically, a little hiss escaping me when the movement pulls at my neck. My top ends up on the floor as well, leaving me completely naked.

"Andre, you're a lucky man."

The gleam of pride in Andre's eyes makes me want to preen. "That I am. Very lucky. Darling, go and show my dear friend Patrick just how lucky I am."

He moves to one side, allowing me to pass. I saunter over to where Patrick is still sitting, my hips rolling. Patrick's gaze follows the movement, the blue of his irises darkening to a vivid indigo ring. A fresh pair of black latex gloves are on his hands—I hadn't realised he'd put them on. He spreads his legs, inviting me to stand between them.

I hold my breath when Patrick lifts his gloved hands, and release it in a shaky exhalation when he brackets my hips just as Andre had done. The rubbery feel of the gloves makes me shudder.

Patrick's eyes follow the path of his hands as they move up to cup my breasts. His thumbs whisk over the tips of my nipples, teasing them into even harder points. Shivery darts of sensation arrow through me, down to my clit, a delicate throb synchronising with my speeding pulse.

"She's very sensitive, isn't she?" Patrick murmurs.

"She is," Andre says. "Exquisitely so."

"Does she mind my touching her?"

My heart flutters at his concern.

Andre laughs, an indulgent chuckle. "Ask her yourself."

"Do you?" Patrick asks me.

His thumbs are resting on my nipples, pressing against them and rotating. It feels likes he winding a crank, tightening something in my belly. It's unbearable. It makes it hard to think. I lick my lips, focusing on expressing my thoughts. "I don't mind," I say, my voice soft and strained. "I like it." A breath shudders from me. My feet shift in a restless little shuffle. "I love it and not just because my Master says so."

Patrick's mouth quirks into a crooked grin. "Good to know." His fingers close on my nipples in a slow pinch. He tugs on them, pulling them out from my body until the pressure makes me hiss, then he releases them completely, watching them bounce pertly back into place. "Beautiful," he murmurs.

Andre steps behind me, his hands slipping round to curl around my ribcage, framing my tits. His suit is cool against my back, his hands and breath hot on my skin. His touch reassures me, grounding me in the moment. A part of me relaxes even as my excitement increases. Nothing bad can happen when Andre touches me and if it's something good—which this definitely is—he will only make it even better.

"She tastes good too," Andre says and Patrick doesn't waste any time in leaning forward and sucking one of my nipples into his mouth.

I moan. My hands curl into fists at my sides. I want to touch him, to thread my fingers through his rumpled looking hair and bring his head even closer to me. I bite my bottom lip to keep from demanding more. Harder, suck harder, I beg from inside my head. I whimper in disappointment when Patrick releases my nipple with a wet pop of sound. I groan in delight when he moves to greedily suck my other nipple into his hot mouth.

Pleasure rakes me, from my chest to pussy. My hips bump forward with the force of its arrival and Andre chuckles into my ear.

"Does it feel good, darling?"

"So good, Sir."

"Do you want more?"

"Yes, Sir." More, more, always more. Hunger aches in the pit of my stomach, a chasm of want that only a big cock and a hard fucking can fill.

Andre chuckles again. "That's my greedy girl." To Patrick he says, "touch her pussy."

Patrick's hand is instantly there, his latex covered fingers sliding through the slippery petals of my cunt. It feels weird, like condom-wearing cocks but smaller of course, more nimble. I imagine tentacles might feel like this. The thought makes me rain honey all over his probing digits.

I moan, opening my legs wider, inviting him inside. Still sucking on my nipple, Patrick slips one of his fingers into me.

My eyes roll with the effort to be still. I want to tilt my head back, rest it on Andre's shoulder, but I can't change position, his order holding me in place.

Patrick moves his finger in me, pumping it in and out as his thumb fans my clit. Unlatching his mouth from my nipple, he glances down, looking at himself as he touches me. We're all watching, Andre looking over my shoulder to watch another man pleasuring me.

"You're so wet." Patrick's voice has become a deep rumble.

I can see his erection stretching down the leg of his jeans. My body clenches around his penetrating finger. He looks big and fat, long.

"And you're so tight," Patrick continues. He adds another finger to the one inside me, thrusting them into me harder. I groan at the stretch, a tremor vibrating through me. Sweat dews on my skin, my temperature soaring. The pleasure is building, a trap poised on the edge of snapping shut. I'm too excited and if I come without permission, I'll be punished.

"Sir," I gasp.

Andre turns his face toward me, his innocent expression sitting uncomfortably over his skull. "Is there something wrong, darling?"

He knows damn well what's wrong. "I'm going to come."

"Are you?" he asks, dark amusement in his voice. "But I haven't said you can yet."

I wail, a thin reedy cry of longing. My body strains with the effort to obey. Patrick's eyes find mine and by the wicked gleam there, I know he's making it as hard for me as possible. His fingers slam into me, his thumb moving in taut circles on my clit. I can't stop shaking, my muscles jumping and twitching beneath my sweat-slicked skin.

"Please." My voice breaks on the word. "Please let me come, Sir."

"What do you think, Patrick? Should we let this sweet girl come?"

"I don't know," Patrick muses. Jamming his fingers into me, he flexes them. Pleasure robs me of breath as he rubs against that sweet, urgent spot inside me. "She hasn't asked me and I'm the one finger-fucking her greedy pussy."

"You heard him, darling," Andre says to me. His fingers pinch my nipples, tugging them in rhythmic pulls. "Ask Patrick if you can come. Ask him nicely."

"Please, Patrick. Please let me come. You feel so

good. I don't think I can hold on," I whimper. The pleasure is so sharp it might as well be pain. "Please. Oh, please. Oh god!" My legs quake, my trembling legs threatening to spill me to the floor.

The two of them laugh, self-satisfied masculine chuckles. I gnash my teeth and my frustration amuses them even more.

"Come then," Patrick smirks. "Come all over my hand."

My body seizes, orgasm crashing over me in a wave of skin-tingling sensation. I scream, pussy clenching in greedy convulsions around Patrick's fingers. He doesn't stop moving them, stretching out my orgasm until black spots swim at the edges of my vision and I feel like I'm going to pass out.

"Beautiful."

Swaying on my feet, held up only by the circle of Andre's arms around me, I blink at Patrick in hazy incomprehension. I moan when he slips his fingers out of me. The wet sound of it makes me blush and the heat in my cheeks deepens when he holds up his gloved hand to show me the plentiful juices covering it. He rubs a wet finger over my mouth, outlining my lips, and groans when I lick them clean with thorough swipes of my tongue.

"I want to fuck her."

Patrick doesn't wait for Andre to answer. His hands tear at the fastenings of his jeans. He winces when he reaches into them and pulls out his dick. I was right—he's big, maybe even a little bigger than Andre, and beautiful. The thick stalk of his shaft rears up from a neatly trimmed nest of dark blond hair, the heavily veined and ruddy flesh gleaming wetly at the tip.

Grabbing hold of my wrists, Patrick pulls me out of Andre's arms and onto his lap. I gasp as I land on top of his cock. The rigid length of him presses against my slit. The lust that abated with my orgasm, surges back to new and brighter life.

I can't help it. I wiggle on Patrick's lap, smearing my honey all over his cock. He's so hard I can feel his pulse throbbing against my sex. I want to feel it inside me.

One of Patrick's hands is anchored on my waist, the other is curled over my ass. He uses it smack the curve of my butt, a sharp reprimand. "Hold still," he rasps, his voice rough with desire. It licks over my senses like velvet. "I want to come in you, not on you."

Andre laughs. "That's right. Take her in hand. My insatiable wife will walk all over you if you don't. Isn't that right, darling?"

My body clamours, "yes, yes, yes," but I only moan, too dazed by my hunger to verbalise an answer.

Patrick lands another slap on my ass. He does it for the pleasure of it because I've been good and stopped moving. He does it again and again, my skin heating beneath his hands. My bottom warms as he peppers it with smacks, and the heat spreads down between my thighs. It feels like I'm melting, my arousal liquefying my flesh and spilling all over his cock wedged between my folds.

"Beg for it," he snarls.

The words spring from my lips, a racehorse bursting free from the gate. "Please give me your cock." Leaning forward, but still mindful of my neck, I kiss his mouth, nibble on that plump lower lip. "I ache to feel you inside me," I whisper against the flesh I have just made damp. Wriggling a hand between us, I wrap it around his dick. My breath hisses out of me. God, he's so hard, so firm in my hand, ripe fruit just about to burst. He echoes the sound, his hips bumping up, pushing his cock into the tunnel I've made.

"Put it in me," I beg. I squeeze him with rhythmic pulses, a foreshadowing of what my pussy will do if he'll just do what I want. "Please. I'll make you feel so good. I promise. I'll make you come so hard."

"You better," he growls, lifting me up. With a happy cry, I position his cock and drive myself down onto his thick length.

"Fuck!"

I wish I could echo him, but I'm drowning in bliss. He is big, huge, his cock stretching my pussy to the point of pain and beyond. It hurts, but it's that delightful kind of hurt I like best.

"How does she feel, Patrick? Good?"

"So fucking good," Patrick groans. "Hold onto her shoulders. I need to lay her down."

Andre's hands curl under my arms, supporting my upper body as Patrick surges to his feet with my legs wrapped around his waist. They lay me across the seat of the tattoo chair, my shoulders and head held immobile by my Master who stares down at me with a wolfish smile.

"Are you enjoying yourself, darling?"

Impaled on a thick cock, I give the only answer I can. "Mm, so much, Sir."

The last word leaves me on a gasp, Patrick's deep

thrust forcing the air out of my body. He wastes no time in fucking me, his hips slamming forward. He drives his cock into me deep and hard, like he's trying batter his way through my body to reach my throat. Each resounding thrust forces pleasure and pain through me, hammering them into my cells. With my butt and my head hanging over the sides of the chair, I can't move. I can only lie there, staring up at Andre's face as he looks down at me, and take it.

Coarse praise spills from Patrick's mouth. "Fucking tight cunt. So hot. So wet." A feral dig of his cock punctuates each word. His gloved hands rove over my body until they find my breasts. He grabs hold of the jiggling mounds, his fingertips digging in hard enough to bruise.

I groan and spread my legs wider, a rush of wetness anointing his shuttling cock.

Andre grins down at me. "Almost there, darling?"

"Almost, Sir. Almost." My breath hitches. Another orgasm is storming its way toward me. My fingers claw at the leather seat beneath me. "Please, Sir."

A beatific smile stretches across Andre's face. "Come then, darling. Squeeze his cock nice and tight. Let me see it."

The orgasm breaks over me and I scream as it swallows me whole.

Above me, Patrick growls as my pussy clenches tight around his dick. He ruts on me, his thrusts becoming impossibly harder, his hips striking my bottom in harsh smacks. My orgasm surges again, and in the middle of it, I feel Patrick wedge himself inside me, his cock jerking as he fills my hungry pussy with his cum.

I don't take my eyes from Andre's face. I let him see the pleasure flooding through me, let him see what his friend is doing to me. I give everything I'm feeling up to him and watch him accept it with a satisfied smile.

One of his hands moves round, hovers over my throat to remind me of what's there now. I'm his, forever.

I smile. Like I could ever forget.

UNCOVERING HEATHER
BY VICTORIA BLISSE

I HATE THE COMMUTE TO WORK. It's long, it's stinky and once I reach the city it's packed. I sit, laptop bag clasped to my chest like a shield and staring fixedly at the floor. I wish I could read, then I'd hide behind the pages of a book but it makes me feel sick so I just appraise shoes instead. Or ignore them, depending on the day.

Today I'm ignoring them, as most are muddied or rain stained. I'm quite aware of my own damp tights inside my sensible work heels so I don't need reminding of the deluge which will greet me when I finally emerge from Liverpool Street Station and walk to work.

And my umbrella broke. It's pink, my favourite colour, and a random vindictive gust blew it inside out until it snapped moments after I left the house but far enough away that I had no time to go back and pick up my waterproof. My drab brown work suit is drab and damp and I'm miserable.

The flame-emblazoned boots come into my line of sight and I can't help but admire them. Thick soles that look like tyre treads for a truck and heavy silver fittings that look like they must weight a ton. They're boots that mean business and the owner sits down next to me.

"Fuck, it's pissing it down out there!"

I don't look up. The voice is low and honeyed and doesn't sound drunk but the first rule of tube travel is 'do not look at a talker who you don't know because you can bet they will talk at you for the duration of the journey and you won't want to hear it'.

"I don't need to tell you that though love, do I?" His touch zaps through me like lightning and I snap my head round to give him my hardest, darkest stare. I hate people getting up in my personal space.

The guy ignores it though and continues to babble.

"But we're Brits, right? Born and bred in this stuff. Makes us stronger and all that."

Why am I still looking at him?

Is it the large, green eyes peering out from beneath the immaculately messed up quiff of black hair on top of his otherwise shaved head? Or the plump lips below them, punctuated by two black studs on the left corner. Or maybe it's the distended ear plugged up with a dragon, its head smiling at me.

"I can tell you're a local. You're not engaging with the crazy guy." He winks and heat explodes in my cheeks.

"No—I—Not—Well—"

"Don't sweat it, I'm used to it." He shrugs.

"Sorry, I'm in an awful mood. My favourite pink umbrella broke on me this morning and now I am completely sodden and have a full day of staring at a computer screen and squelching in my shoes to look forward to." God, this guy has got me disturbed. I just told him way more personal detail about myself than I'm comfortable with.

"Well that fucking sucks but hey, the universe has brought you the gift of me to make up for it. I'm Jet by the way."

Jet holds out his hand and I notice the intricate red rose tattoo peeking out from the edge of his leather, studded jacket and extending up to his knuckles which I find myself gripping. It might be the Brit in me. You have to complete a handshake, it'd be rude not too.

"I'm Heather." The smile radiates across my face and I don't know why. I don't like piercings, I don't like tattoos and I certainly don't like strangers who touch and talk to me on the tube so why am I warming to this one? I hold my hand out and he takes it firmly in his. Which is hot, his grip hard but giving.

"What a beautiful name. Mind you, I might be biased. I was brought up in the Yorkshire moors so I know how glorious heather can be when in full bloom."

I feel like I'm blooming, my cheeks are certainly pink from his compliment and his touch. Why hasn't he let go of my hand yet?

"Erm, thanks, Jet."

He smiles, turns my hand in his and lays a kiss on the back of it, I can feel the sharp coldness of his piercings and the warmth of his lips and I can't think, don't remember how to breathe and seem to be lost in the depth of his warm green eyes.

"Charmed." His smile is leisurely yet intense and seems to warm me from ear to ear and then down to my toes.

Jet lets go of my hand with a jolt.

"Oh, I love your earrings." He leans in and squints at my earlobe. "Yeah, yeah, thought so. They're barn owls aren't they?"

"Yeah," I nod, "pink ones. It's my favourite colour and I love owls."

"Me too, my favourite tattoo is of a Barn owl, wanna see it?"

"Sure," I squeak, not sure if I really do, but carried away by his enthusiasm.

"I got it done a few years ago," he grabs at the neck of the black and white skull decorated t-shirt beneath his jacket and pulls the neck down lower with both hands, stretching it to reveal a good chunk of his chest which is emblazoned with a realistic barn owl with wings spread, eyes focused on me.

"It's stunning," I murmur, looking left and right at the other commuters gawping at us. I'd like to study it closer, stroke it, find out what other bits of him are covered in ink. I think I'm attracted to the crazy tattooed man. How the hell did that happen?

The tube pulls to a stop and I look at the sign, it's Moorgate, the end of my journey is in sight.

"Jet, I have to go, well, the next stop is mine." I genuinely wish I didn't have to go to work, thought about calling in sick and just riding the rails with the lunatic I only met five minutes ago. I must be insane.

"Really? Well that's a fucking shame." He sighs.

That's another thing I hate, casual swearing. Mum

would say it was the sign of a weak mind. I can't even think swear words without imagining my mum looking down her nose at me from Heaven. I'm a grown woman but I can't break free of the rules she set for me even now.

I break from my thoughts to see Jet patting around his pockets, on his coat then his torn jeans.

"Ah, knew I had it." He pulls out a pencil, looks like eyeliner actually. Is Jet wearing makeup? Before I can examine him further he's grabbing my hand and rolling up my sleeve. "I'll write it up here on your wrist so it doesn't wear off." He grins.

"I've got paper," I gasp, as he turns my hand and presses the pencil tip to my skin.

"No time, beautiful." He scrawls his numbers and pulls down my sleeve again.

"Call me, yeah?"

I nod, stand and walk away from him on very unsteady legs. Stepping onto the platform I look back at the tube window and there he is, twisted in his seat and looking right at me. Casually he waves and I find myself waving back until the train whirs back into life and disappears down the tunnel.

My mind often wanders when I'm at work. It's not a challenge, filling spreadsheets with figures, writing up cover letters and responding to boringly repetitive emails. Today I can't concentrate at all. I keep being distracted by lush green eyes and a barn owl in flight. How on earth can I be attracted to a man like that?

I like my men squeaky clean, smart suits and cut glass accents. I like my life clean cut come to that. I don't like things messed up; I make my bed every morning, wash the dishes the moment I've eaten a meal. I iron every item of my clothing, even my knickers. I don't suppose Jet's ironed anything in his life.

His digits seemed to burn on my flesh though. I should just wash them off, I'll never ring him, we're too different. There's nothing we could possibly have in common. I mean I used to visit Yorkshire as a kid. Dad loved camping and he loved the dales and the moors. I've spent many a windswept hour walking through the heather but that's not something you build a relationship on.

Relationship? God, we've not got enough to form a friendship, not really. It was a strange little meeting on a wet morning. It was a distraction, a tale to tell of the madness of London life. Nothing more.

The commute home is boring. There's no sign of the tattooed crazy and it's still raining. So when I eventually walk through my front door I'm cold, wet and miserable. I peel off each layer of clothing and throw it all in the washing machine. As I scoop out the powder I glimpse my wrist. The black is still there, smudged but visible.

Some compulsion makes me type the number into my phone. I save it, shake my head and walk the short way to my bathroom. A studio flat is small by definition, my London studio flat is more like a cupboard.

The hot water beats against my skin and as I run my hands over my flesh I remember how excited I was when Jet touched me, when he kissed the back of my hand. How excited would I be if he kissed me elsewhere? Rubbing scented gel over my breasts I remember his owl lying over his chest. So realistic, so beautiful. What is the story behind it? Why is it forever emblazoned across his skin?

What else does he have? I saw glimpses of a tattoo around his neck of all places, and that intricate rose on the back of his hand. He'd never be able to hide them behind clothes. So where does he work? Does he even work?

Determined to stop thinking about the annoying man I throw on my fleecy pyjamas and open a bottle of wine. Guilt stabs in the pit of my stomach. Drinking on a work night, it's definitely a rebellious act. It's not responsible. It's probably the first step on the slippery slope to hell but for once I ignore the imagined aberration of my dead mother and pour myself a large glass of red and settle down in my bed to watch some mindless telly.

I'm quite surprised when I look at my glass and there's only a drop left in the bottom. How've I finished two glasses of wine already? Glancing at the clock I realise it's well past my bedtime, down the last sip and pick up my mobile phone.

It's still on the screen with Jet's number.

I like your ink.

I type and hit send. Why not? It's a perfectly innocent message and he probably won't reply. I'm not even sure I copied the number down correctly anyway.

Well thanks. Who are you?

Shit, he responded. I giggle out loud. I'm not supposed to swear not even think it. How much bloody wine have I drunk?

Heather. From the tube.

Makes me sound like toothpaste. I roll around the bed laughing until my mobile tinkles.

Ah, beautiful Heather, I was hoping it was you.

The letters tip tap from my fingers and I send before I think.

Really?

Drunk texting. Now I'm really not being clever. I should just put it on silent and go to sleep.

I've been thinking about you all day. Wanna meet for coffee?

I shouldn't respond. I should sleep.

Yeah, do you know Polo Bar by Liverpool Street Station?

I finally turn off the sound, set my alarm and ready for sleep. His reply pops up seconds later.

Know it well. What time?

Thinking I should really be asleep I send a time, close the pink cover on my phone, shut my eyes and drift off.

See you at six, beautiful Heather x

The message stares at me on and off all day. I'm not going to meet him, can't possibly. Several times I start a text back to make an excuse but just can't find a way to turn him down that doesn't look awful.

I'm determined just to stand him up, he probably won't even be there anyway. Guys like Jet don't court ladies like me. Why I walk into the café instead of walking past it I don't know. The more surprising thing is that he's there.

"Beautiful Heather!" He cries from the booth at the back making heads turn and appraise me. My cheeks flare and I wave hesitantly at Jet before walking over to join him. He's wearing a dark denim shirt, unbuttoned at the top to show off the entirety of his inked neck. It's a wolf, stylised, square, maw open and eyes piercing. This man is a walking canvas.

He stands and as I approach he wraps his arms around me.

I hesitantly return his hug. I'm British, we don't show such affection to virtual strangers. He holds me tight and for longer than I'm comfortable with. He can feel every extra inch of wobble on my well-padded frame and that frightens the hell out of me.

"I'm so happy to see you again," he exclaims and I mumble something non-committal into his chest. He's a good head taller than me even in my heels and definitely strong. Just as I wonder if panic will make me scream he pulls back and I instantly miss his warmth. Damn my indecisive mind.

"What do you want?" He asks, settling himself back down on the wooden bench, backed by dazzling white tiles. I slide in the one opposite him.

"Erm, a tea please, thanks."

He nods at a waitress who comes over, takes the order with a smile and strides off.

Now what am I going to do?

"I knew you'd contact me." Jet says, casually tapping his fingers on the table top.

"You did? That's impressive because I didn't."

"Mm," he nods. "I saw it in your eyes."

"You're a bit full of yourself," I snap.

"Oh, believe you me I'm not, but life's too short to fuck about."

Just then the waitress returns with a tall mug of coffee for him and a tea pot, cup and mini milk bottle for me. We both divert from conversation to attend to our hot beverages. Why am I so riled by his confidence? Maybe I'm just scared. I don't know what he might do next and I like to be in control.

"I'm glad you texted, Heather, truly. I like you. Liked you from the moment I saw you, do you want to know why?"

"Yeah," I nod, wrapping my fingers around the wide cup, feeling the heat warm my palms.

"Because on the outside you look like every other drab drone, toeing the line, enduring the daily grind to make another dollar. Making this capitalistic machine work but inside you're not like that."

I crinkle my brows.

Drone? How dare he!

"Inside is a secret rebel. I saw it in the cute bows on your plain work shoes, and the cool owls at your ears. Definitely not sensible work wear and the luscious pink silk lining of your jacket when I folded it back to leave you my number. And that is the bit of you that's curious about me I bet."

Well, I can't deny it, I'm certainly curious about him.

"So go on then, ask me anything. I'm an open book." He takes a long sip of his coffee, fixing me with his intense stare through the steam.

"Where do you work?"

"I'm an illustrator, a designer, a kind of artist. I'm independent so I work at home. How about you?"

"Just a boring office job. Admin and general dog's body. I hate it."

"Why do you do it then?" He asks.

"Because I need the money," I reply a little more sneeringly than I intended.

He shrugs and runs a hand through his lazily quiffed curls.

"Why do you have a rose on the back of your hand?"

"Oh, my Gran was called Rose. It's to remember her. She was always there to support me, always there to hold my hand." He looks down on the rose wistfully and it pulls at my heartstrings.

"That's a lovely tribute. I don't think I could ever have a tattoo."

"Why not?"

"Because I'm a coward and my Mum hated them, said that only sailors and ne'er do wells have them."

"I don't like to speak ill of the dead but your mum sounds like she was a bit of a prick."

"She was." I agreed. There's no use denying it. She controlled me from the moment I was born until the moment she died. "But I still find it hard to not live by her rules."

"Because you're a good girl, Heather. I can see that and you could be great if you just believed in yourself a little more."

"How dare you judge me!" I snap. He poked me directly in my sore spot.

"I'm not, love, believe you me I'd not dare. I'm just saying what I see written all over your face."

"Why do you do that?" I ask, "just say what you're thinking."

"Because there's too many two-faced twats in the world, Heather and what you see with me is what you get. No pretences, no heirs and graces. That shit's not worth it."

"And why do you swear so much?"

"Because you don't fucking like it." He smiles, a wicked glint in his eye.

"And why do you want to disturb me?"

"Because I want to see past your barriers and into your soul."

I gulp. No one has ever wanted to see my soul before.

"I don't think there's much—"

"Stop right there, Heather," He puts a hand over mine on the table. "Don't even dare to put yourself down."

"But—"

"No. I won't hear it. Ask me another question, go on, then I've got one for you."

"Okay, why do you say I've got barriers up when you clearly have too?"

"Oh, touché," Jet laughs and nods his head approvingly. "We all need our safe spaces to function. I look like this because I get an instant reaction that tells me what a person is like. I face judgement and prejudice every day but choose to turn my back on it. Now it's my turn. Would you like to come back to my place and fuck?"

I open my mouth ready to shoot him down but I can't get the words out so I flounder, mouth open, finger raised with nothing to say. My world is filled with niceties and false politeness. My life has been a construct made from fear, lies and guilt and finally someone has broken through everything that's held me back and seen through to the me trapped deep inside, the pink loving rebel longing for freedom.

"Jet, it rather scares me but yes, I think I would."

"Come on then love, I don't live far away."

I shuck my coat on in a bit of a daze and follow Jet down the tight corridor between tables in the busy 24-hour café. He pauses at the till and pays the bill. I don't even protest, just follow him out the door.

"It's just a few minutes' walk, beautiful Heather, you up for it?"

"The walk?" I ask, without thinking. He laughs heartily and slips his arm over my shoulder.

"Yes the walk love, we've already established what you're up for once we get to mine."

"Yeah, about that." His touch makes me tingle but his quiet confidence can't shut up the blind panic that is now partying in the depths of my stomach. "I'm not sure why I said yes, I don't do this kind of thing. It's not like me at all."

"Chill, Heather, I'm no monster. I understand consent. You can change your mind at any time, love." His arm is still over my shoulders and he squeezes me to him.

"Okay, Jet, I don't understand anything when I'm with you."

He leans in and casually kisses the corner of my hairline.

"That's because you're thinking too much. Stop thinking and listen to your gut. It'll make it so much simpler."

My gut is currently turning cartwheels and being of no help whatsoever. I feel like I'm going to be sick at any moment but there's a joy whizzing through my veins that I can't deny. It's like running round and round in a revolving door. Fun and nauseating all at the same time.

Jet keeps talking all the way to his flat. I'm listening, taking in snippets. He doesn't demand any response which is good because I'm not sure I'm capable of forming words. He keeps touching me. For a while we'll walk side by side and then he'll grab my hand or put his palm on the small of my back or hug my shoulders again. The guy can't stop touching me.

I don't want him to.

His flat is similar in size to mine but there the similarity ends. The walls are covered in graffiti, giant versions of tattoos, words, animals, trees, birds, flowers. Even the ceiling is decorated. The bed is unmade, there are pots in the sink. It's not a tip by any stretch of the imagination, but there's a careless messiness to everything that makes my skin itch. I hold back the urge to tidy. Although knowing what I do of Jet he wouldn't mind.

"Make yourself comfy love, I'll be back in a jiff."

I look round the room several times but there's nothing for it. I'm going to have to sit on the bed. I perch genteelly on the very edge of the mattress. What the hell am I doing here?

"Oh, I said make yourself comfortable." He laughs, bursting out of the bathroom like he's just walked on stage at a rock concert. He rips the buttons open on his shirt and throws it over his shoulder so it lands crumpled on the floor before throwing himself at the bed and me.

I scream as his arm catches me and he pushes me flat on the bed.

"What the—" I squeak, trying to scrabble into a sitting position but his arm is stubbornly pinning me down.

"Lighten up, Heather, this isn't meant to be serious you know." He blows a raspberry on my cheek.

"Oh, fuck off." I shake my head and push myself out of his embrace. The crazy bleeding psycho throwing himself at me like that.

Jet laughs, deep and hearty.

"Now there you are. I knew you were in there somewhere."

He sits up and places a hand over mine, poised as I am to push myself off the bed and out of his life.

"Come on, Heather, I want to see more of you, need to see more of you."

"Jet," I'm lost in the depths of his wide, sparkling eyes. "I'm not sure I can do this, can be what you want me to be."

"I only want you to be yourself," he smiles and cups my face in his large hand. "But the door is there. I can't make you do anything you don't want to do. Wouldn't want to."

And there it is, that small, inexplicable voice in my heart whispering for me to give him a chance.

"Tell me about your tattoos." I reply. I don't know why; my attraction to him doesn't make any sense.

"Okay, I'll start at the beginning."

Taking my hand in his, he presses it to his heart.

"This is Barney. I got him when I was just eighteen. I'd saved for years. I knew what I wanted. Owls are silent, they own the night, they're wise and free. Everything I longed to be."

Under his hand I spread my fingers and trace the intricate feathers, feeling the warmth of his skin beneath the ink.

"I love owls," I whisper, tracing the line of the wings, Jet's hand no longer covering mine. "They're such ethereal creatures, mystical and fascinating." I lean in closer, the eyes of the beast are so sharp and calculating. I do something impulsive and kiss the inked beak gently. I feel the growl against my lips more than I hear it.

"The next one was the rose on my hand, for my Gran. She died when I was twenty. I had the rose done the day after her funeral."

I turn my gaze to his right hand then take it in my own.

"Would she have liked it do you think?" I trace the petals from the centre, out.

"Oh, yeah, she loved my artwork. I designed her this, she had it hung on her wall, in a frame. She'd love the tattoo. I added the thorns for the grief I felt. Not just for Gran, other losses and pains."

"Are your emotions all painted over your body?" Kissing the back of his hand I trace up onto his wrist, turn it and kiss all around, covering the thorns of grief.

"A lot of them. Childhood joy is just up from there. My Luck Dragon tattoo is a memory from my favourite kid's film. You know, having a Luck Dragon is the only way to go on a quest. And my life is a quest."

I trace the beautiful dragon, as it twists around his arm.

"I had the background filled in, the hills and mountains, the eternal sunrise and the beautiful blue sky breaking through the clouds. I had my sleeve completed with the night sky that overlaps my owl when I was twenty-five."

"Doesn't it hurt?" I ask, kissing up his arm to the shoulder.

"Yeah, but I just kinda zone it out. It's not bad pain. It's constructive, therapeutic."

"I think you're addicted."

"Might be. Got my wolf next to top off my totem."

I continue my kisses up to the neck piece, he cranes his head back so I can see it properly.

"It's a fierce statement." I pepper kisses through the ruffled fur and bared teeth, "didn't you worry about it being so visible?"

"No," he coughs as I pause and suck a patch of naked skin just below his ear. I'm enjoying my leisurely exploration. "It's me. I'm a lone wolf, howling at the moon and standing out from the crowd. If you don't like Wolfie, you won't like me."

"Wolfie?" I lift my lips from his skin and giggle.

"Yes, I name all my animal tattoos."

"Very imaginative." I nod, eyes widening in mirth.

"Oh here's the naughty girl," Jet purrs and stills my giggles with his lips. There's no soft introduction, his mouth possesses mine and soon I'm groping round for something to hold on to, blasted by the intensity of his kiss. I find his chest and slide my hands down to his sides, needing to grip more tightly. "I want to see more."

He rips the jacket down my arms roughly, I'd yell normally—this cost me a fortune, it's personally tailored—but I want to feel his hands on me. He throws it to the floor then starts on the buttons of my blouse. Before I know it I'm sitting in just my boring work bra and skirt and he's devouring every inch of my skin with his gaze and then with his hands and his kisses.

We're doing this, we're really doing this. Jet reaches round and unfastens my bra as I scatter kisses over his chest, his hands are wide and knowing, they touch and tease and flow over my skin. All the doubts and fears are melting away in the flow of lust that captivates me.

This time when he pushes me to the bed I don't resist, and he drags down my skirt without protest and the fuchsia knickers beneath it.

"What is it about pink?" He asks me as he pulls at the zip of his trousers, leaving me alone and exposed. My heart hammers. What the hell am I doing?

"It's my favourite colour," I reply, fidgeting against the sheets. When he's with me I'm lost in him, now he's hopping about trying to get off his boot I'm shaking with nerves for when he looks back at me.

"That's not it," he shakes his head, boot finally in hand. "It's more than that."

I shrug, wrapping my arms around my body, curling round to hide myself.

"I wasn't allowed to wear pink, it was too suggestive."

"There it is." He turns back to me, completely

naked bar a satisfied smile.

"No, no, Heather," he leaps onto the bed beside me. "Don't cover up your beautiful canvas."

"Do you want to tattoo me?" I gasp as he takes hold of my hand and presses it back against the mattress.

"No, not my talent, but I want to paint you."

"Paint me? I'm no work of art." I shake my head as he prizes my other hand over my head too, splitting my thighs and kneeling between them. I can't hide myself from him now.

"Oh, you are," he growls, "and I'm going to paint you from head to toe. Starting here."

He kisses my nose making me giggle.

"You are beautiful." Each cheek is peppered with kisses. "Your skin my canvas, my kisses my paint."

His lips hit mine and I kiss him back with a fierceness that brings tears to my eyes. I've not felt beautiful in a long time; with this handsome, crazy man I can almost believe that I am.

"Beautiful Heather," he murmurs, kissing my chin and my neck, hands still in mine, holding me down, holding me open. "You're a gift."

His lips are soft, his piercings a unique part of his kiss. I catch my breath as he lowers, skimming over my chest and down to the natural seat of my large breasts. He looks up at me, mouth poised between my cleavage and he looks hungry.

Removing his grip, he employs both hands to gather up my ample bosom. He dives right in, kissing and kneading, slurping and moaning. I am devoured and I laugh as his stubble tickles my flesh and the joyful lust transmits from him to me.

Jet revels in every inch of me and it's a powerful aphrodisiac that buzzes through my veins until I'm writhing beneath him and moaning. The chains that bound me, the expectations and the fears all melt away as he caresses and kisses even lower. He doesn't skim over the soft roundness of my stomach, he delights in it as much as he did my breasts, tickling my belly button with his tongue until I roar with laughter.

Which is surprisingly sexy. I'm more turned on than I've ever been in my life before and when he finally reaches the centre of my thighs and opens me up, I know I am wet and hot, and although I flush with heat as he inspects me, I don't feel shame. I am beautiful Heather, he thinks so, there's no point me denying it.

He is a noisy and messy eater. It's so intimate, so much of a turn on to have his face there, pressed flat against my most intimate folds, his tongue seeking out moisture, finding my clit, lapping and lashing, his lips sucking, fingers probing.

My orgasm hits with an explosion and a never before experienced gush so powerful that it shakes my body from top to toe. He laps and licks and groans sucking down what he can.

"Nectar," he gasps, clambering to his knees. "Can I fuck you?"

His cock is hard and I can't take my eyes off its ridges and dips.

"No," I gasp, surprising myself, "I want to fuck you."

He lets out a short, staccato laugh and rolls to the bed beside me.

"Whatever you want, love." He winks.

I clamber over him, eager to feel him inside.

"I want to be able to see your art as we fuck," I explain guiding his erection into me. I stop to groan as he stretches and fills me so intimately.

"You haven't told me about all of them yet."

"No," he gasps, thrusting his hips up as I fully impale myself on him. "No, I haven't."

"What tattoo was next?" I bite my bottom lip and try to keep my eyes open, to look down on him, on his artwork, on his beautiful, lithe body.

"The white tiger and the panther."

I look at them, one either side of his belly button, raised up on back paws, fore paws paused mid-lunge. Both beasts growling.

He grips my hips and I grind harder against him. I flick my gaze higher and his eyes are tightly closed.

"What are they for?"

"The battle within," he replies simply. "Good, bad, truth, lies, all there. In my totem."

Everything he has ever experienced is there, patchworked on his skin. He's so open. I've spent a life hiding away. I don't want that any more. I want to be Jet's beautiful Heather, fuck convention.

"So," I groan, trying hard to focus on the last tattoo, "what about the elephant?"

He stands stoic between the fighting tiger and panther. Forming the base of the totem of tattoos up the centre of Jet's body.

"He is strength. He is reliability and longevity. He is what I want at the centre of it all. To live a full life. To be seen, to be uniquely and instantly identifiable, to not be able to hide."

"I want that," I grind harder on him, faster, as his grip tightens and his body flexes and tenses. "I don't want to hide anymore."

He opens his eyes, it's a strain, I can tell. He's close to coming.

"There you are." He grunts each word and then roars my name as he folds up into me, holding me, pulling me down against his chest. We untangle and re-tangle in each other. Gasping, panting and kissing.

"Beautiful Heather," he sighs, "I think I've finally found you."

"Handsome Jet, you've not uncovered all of me yet."

"Not yet, no, but I look forward to taking my time doing it."

VENOMOUS INK
BY ALAIN BELL

SCARLETT HARNESSES ALL TWELVE YEARS of her experience to keep her hand steady. Not only is she distracted by touching the Mona Lisa of breasts, but the gorgeous woman—Amalie—is moaning and squirming under the effects of her gun.

It's not like this is the first time that a client squirmed, twitched, or jerked while she's working on them. It's not the first time she has worked on parts of the human body normally hidden by clothing. Nor is it the first time that a client moaned, cried, or screamed. It's not even the first time a client gained pleasure from the bite of the tattoo needles. It is however, the first time that it has culminated together in someone with such a perfect form and so sensuously sexy as the woman under her gun.

From what she can tell, Amalie is deep in sub-space. Not that Scarlett knows if she's a sub, but the exquisite woman is at least in that happy place where pain becomes a sensuous caress. A fine sheen of sweat covers her client's skin. She's breathing in quick deep gasps, her chest rising and falling in a steady rhythm that allows Scarlett to keep constant pressure with her needles despite the movement.

Event through the black nitrile gloves, her skin feels amazing. Warm, vital and alive. Over the entire session Scarlett has had to keep herself from inappropriately stroking the woman. The attraction is almost a force of nature. Only her professionalism prevents her from ravishing the woman on the table.

And the session's not easy. Amalie's skin is stubborn about absorbing the special ink, so Scarlett has to make several passes over already aggravated skin. And whatever this pigment is, it seems to be stingier than normal tattoo ink. She could tell that Amalie was in quite a bit of pain before she went into subspace. But Scarlett can't argue with the results. The ink creates the most beautiful colors she has seen, giving her art an additional life she can only envy.

Amalie's hips are undulating in a slow primal rhythm of their own. The aroma of the sensual woman's arousal mixes with the ambient smell of bleach, antiseptic, and lidocaine cleanser. Her trousers are unbuttoned and unzipped, exposing her lacy blue panties. The thin strip of satin covering her sex is just visible and clearly damp. Scarlett is glad she chose to start at the abdomen and work her way up to the breasts. Being that close to the intoxicating scent is challenging; she does her best to ignore the warmth and dampness in her own core.

The woman warned Scarlett this would happen, and she just waved it off. Now she wishes that she had given the warning more credence. Amalie paid extra to complete the tattoo all in one sitting, even going so far as to bring bite-sized food and a fork for Scarlett, and a large protein infused drink for herself.

Amalie insisted that pauses be as short as possible once she hit subspace and Scarlett kept to her promise. No pause has been longer than three minutes as she simply stretched her hands back, took a bite of her savory meal, and fed Amalie some of her drink through the angled straw. The woman drank automatically, never leaving her special world.

The goddess on Scarlett's table is an enigma.

***

She came in looking the classic bookish woman. She wore a gray tailored trouser suit with a white blouse buttoned to her neck. Her red hair was tied in a bun on top of her head, and secured with wooden hair sticks carved in an intricate Celtic knot-work pattern. Anachronistic glasses completed the look and accentuated her blue eyes while also hiding her stunning beauty. Scarlett wondered at the affectation. Eye correction was perfected a few years ago in 2026.

During their consultation Amalie revealed she had done her research. She specifically sought Scarlett out for her skill and speed at photo-realistic depictions of wildlife. She made sure Scarlett was willing to work with the photo and ink she supplied and would do the large piece in one sitting. Additionally, she requested a ride home after as she knew she would be in no shape to drive.

Her last request almost ended the transaction right there until Amalie placed her warm hand on Scarlett's and said, "Please. And feel free to set up any safety measures that will make you feel safe; even bring a bodyguard if you like. I'll pay for their time as well."

Her willingness to offer protection was the extra bit that convinced Scarlett. If Amalie was willing to suggest extra security, she either had no ulterior motives in mind or the response would be so extreme that Scarlett wouldn't be safe even in the shop. Her instincts made her think the former and believe the woman harmless.

In another show of trust, Amalie paid in full upfront, and showed an envelope of cash that contained a thirty percent tip. She arrived for the session in attire similar to their first meeting, but this time in blue with a contrasting aqua shirt, again buttoned to her neck.

Once inside Scarlett's private room, she began the preparation while Amalie took off her upper clothing. When she heard Amalie lay on the bench she turned and froze at the sight before her. She had never seen someone so beautiful in her life. The bulky conservative suits hid a slender athletic body. Small but perfect breasts rose proudly on her chest, only minimally flattened by the pull of gravity. Natural but still firm, topped by perfect-sized rosy pink nipples. Her skin that is uninked is smooth and invites a caress. Scarlett wanted nothing more than to lick and nibble on her flat but soft looking belly.

The woman wasn't a tattoo virgin. Intricate emerald green tattoos resembling Celtic knots covered both her arms in a three quarters sleeve. They weren't quite Celtic, more like electronic circuits with patterns mimicking words and symbols. She'd never seen anything so detailed and perfect for someone's form. The strokes didn't detract from the curves and muscles of her arms, and only drew Scarlett's eyes to follow the lines and appreciate the beauty and complexity of the human limbs. Each sleeve was different, but the asymmetry only added to the appeal.

She saw the tops of tattoos on the parts of Amalie's thighs that were exposed by the open trousers. The artwork was similar to that on her arms. Another path lead from the tattoos on her legs, over her hips and ribs, to connect to the arm sleeves.

Her torso was pristine except for three colorful tattoos. Complex circular patterns anointed her breastbone, solar plexus, and her abdomen below her belly button. Each was a unique design that seemed both mystical and electronic. The art on the heart chakra was green; its lines and curves brought thoughts of love and family to Scarlett's mind. Confidence and power emanated from the yellow plexus chakra and the pattern on the sacral chakra gave energy to Scarlett's hands, just the sight of it sent a lightning bolt of desire through her.

A tinkling giggle snapped her out of her reverent perusal of Amalie's body. As she dragged her gaze upwards, she swore she could see another ornamental blue circle on her throat, but as soon as she saw it, it was gone. All thought of the circle vanished from her mind as her stare continued upwards and lit on Amalie's pale-pink smiling lips. She had to resist the urge to lean forward and kiss the woman until she forgot why she was there.

When her gaze continued over the small pert nose,

she saw another confusing flash of an indigo-colored circle of lines on the woman's forehead. The image also disappeared before she could comprehend it. Working upwards, she met Amalie's eyes and fell into their sapphire blue depths.

***

Scarlett snaps out of her memories to concentrate on her work. Thinking about the woman that way could only lead to trouble. With a capital T. She will remain professional, no matter the attraction. She's almost done with the lifelike blue Malaysian coral snake. Its five-foot length seems to slither along Amalie's form, tail resting near her right hip and dipping under the sacral pattern as it moves low across her abdomen. The rest of its body weaves around the existing art, and over her right breast to curve back and spiral around her left. The head she's working on finishes with its mouth open, fangs poised to bite her nipple.

The thrusting of Amalie's hips increases as the needles sting her areola. Somehow, even in her subspace, the woman controls herself so only her fast deep breathing moves her chest while her pelvis pumps and rotates with abandon.

Nearly complete, Scarlett takes another break. All that remains are the fangs. The ink Amalie supplied shimmers with so much vibrancy that the scales seem alive. If it wasn't impossible, she would swear that the snake is breathing. It must be the movement of the writhing woman.

She gives Amalie another sip that the woman sucks down without any indication of being aware she's doing so. There are only two nuggets remaining of the savory-sweet teriyaki chicken. She snags one with her fork and eats it, amazed at how the flavors are still incredible after the eleven hours of grueling work.

Scarlett doesn't speak, but when she begins the painful white inking of the fangs Amalie begins chanting. What Scarlett hears makes no sense and she almost falters. The chanting sounds like mathematics. Amalie's tone is reverent, and her cadence musical, almost like she's praying, but the language is formulae and numbers.

Scarlett continues her art. The light rhythmic voice of the woman under her gun fills Scarlett with energy and comfort. The sound spurs her on and creativity flows through her fingers.

The instant the needle strikes the last drop of white into the perfect pale skin, Amalie screams. The scream isn't one of pain, but of someone having a shattering orgasm. Scarlett pushes her stool back as the scent of sex permeates the small room and the woman on the table loses her iron control and writhes in sensuous pleasure.

Then the impossible happens, Scarlett drops her tattoo gun. The snake writhes a single path around Amalie's body before returning to its home in the exact position she placed it. She blinks but the snake doesn't move again.

She rubs over her eyes and looks once more. It's still just a tattoo. Maybe eleven hours is too much for one sitting.

She retrieves her gun and examines it for damage while Amalie comes down from her orgasmic high.

Nothing broken, she lays it on the side table and sprays the lidocaine-antiseptic cleanser over the newly-tattooed area of the relaxed but still panting woman. She wipes over a perfectly healed tattoo; the shock of seeing it like that almost causes her to drop the bottle but Amalie covers her hand.

Scarlett looks into the brilliant but faded blue eyes of the ravishing woman. Amalie speaks, her voice weak and rough. "Take me home, and come in for a drink. I'll explain there."

Scarlett can't make her brain work. "But—"

"Please." Amalie squeezes her hand.

Scarlett snaps her mouth shut and gazes into Amalie's comforting sapphire pools. After a few moments her brain calms and she can think. She has questions, but now that the freak out is done she can be calm.

Did the snake really move?

She shakes her head to clear the thought then nods.

Amalie smiles gratefully. "I'll rest while you finish cleaning." Her eyes close, and her body all but melts into the table. "If I drift off, please wake me when you're ready to leave."

***

Scarlett helps the still wobbly Amalie up the stairs to her small two-storey shotgun style house. She can't get a good look at it in the dark. The paint, whatever color it is, is not peeling and the lawn is well maintained, though due for another trim. A rocker sits on the small porch and a flowering plant hangs above the railing, making it look homely.

Amalie misses the lock a few times before she gets her key in and opens the door. She steps in but Scarlett pauses at the stoop.

"Well, you're home safe." Scarlett shoves her hands in her pockets. "Have a good evening."

Amalie reaches back and puts a light hand on Scarlett's elbow. "Please. Come in."

Scarlett looks at her feet; she wants to come in. Unlike Amalie, her arousal at the tattoo session had no release and while she really wants to take the other woman on her entry floor it would be taking advantage. She resigns herself to another night with Rosie Palmer and two of her five sisters. "I shouldn't. You need to recover. And you're a client."

Amalie pulls on her arm. "Please, Scarlett. Please come in." She steps into her personal space and presses a quick chaste peck on her lips.

The smell of clove and ozone tickle Scarlett's nose, along with the scent of sweat and arousal from the session. She touches her tingling lips and looks into the face of the woman that she's drawn to. Amalie's expression is pleading and calming at the same time.

Scarlett's conflicted, but allows herself to be pulled into the house. Amalie presses her to stand in front of a mirror across from the open arch of the living room as she closes the door and locks it. She addresses the air, "Margaret. Lock, security level two. Lights living room. Allow Scarlett to exit when she wishes. Additionally, allow level one actions, and give warning for level two and higher actions. Alert me, no counter measures. Scan now."

A red laser from the mirror scans Scarlett from toes

to head and she almost jumps out of her skin. She jerks again when a subsonic pulse of sound thumps in her chest. A soothing electronic female voice speaks from no identifiable source, as if the house itself is talking. "Scan complete. Welcome Scarlett." The origin of the voice moves so it seems it's coming from Amalie. "Should I make anything to drink Amalie?"

"Yes. Please. Two mochas." Amalie turns to Scarlett who is staring at her, slack-jawed. "Is mocha okay?"

Scarlett wonders if she fell into the rabbit hole. She nods, bewildered at what's going on.

The disembodied voice speaks again "Are you sure you want caffeine this late?"

"Yes, Margaret. If I need to sleep I'll purge the caffeine. For now, I need the boost." Amalie looks at Scarlett. "Do you need to use the facilities?"

Scarlett shakes her head. She doesn't trust herself to speak. So much weirdness is happening. She wants to bolt, but she also wants to know more about what's going on.

Know Amalie.

Wait. Where did that come from? She knows she lusts after the woman. Who wouldn't after seeing that body? But she wants more.

Amalie leads Scarlett into the living room, the electronic voice following. "As you wish."

Amalie says something and walks away, but Scarlett is too in her own head to hear it.

What is this woman? The impossible keeps happening. Is she talking to a computer? It seems so much like a person. The voice can't be A.I. Scientists still haven't pushed anything to this point, have they?

Maybe it's just a good program. Like that Eliza thing she heard about from one of her techie friends. Or was it Turing? Whatever.

She should be terrified, but she isn't. Startled. Amazed. But not scared. Her instincts are rarely wrong, and they are telling her that this woman is safe. More than safe. For some reason... important.

And damn she's sexy. The thought brings another wave of arousal to her core and she shifts, pulling her pants away from her aching center just as Amalie walks into the room with their drinks.

The redhead's lips curl up and eyes crinkle in a satisfied smile. She sits next to Scarlett on the plush sofa, offering her a coffee mug. "Be careful with your drink, and don't be surprised. What I have to tell you sounds impossible, but I promise it's real."

Scarlett nods. A shiver of trepidation skitters up her spine, but the feeling of importance keeps her rooted to her seat. Whilst out the room, Amalie had changed into a loosely bound silky robe. The black cloth contrasts with her skin and clings to her shape. The opening dips well into her cleavage, allowing Scarlett to glimpse part of the snake and an alluring expanse of perfect breasts.

The garment only reaches mid-thigh. The shapely flesh of both legs is covered in an intricate pattern similar to those on Amalie's arms; the design becoming sparser as it continues over her feet. The lines wrap around the sides and Scarlett suspects that the art is even on her soles.

Amalie's voice breaks Scarlett from her perusal of the heavily-tattooed mouthwatering flesh. "I'm a techno-mage."

Despite the earlier warning, Scarlett almost spills her drink. Mage? Magic? "Wait, magic? Are you saying magic is real?"

Amalie raises a hand and waves it in the air. "Yes and no. There are forces that most people don't understand, and ways to control them. The effects have the semblance of magic, but not everyone can control these forces, even if they know of them. It takes a certain... something."

"Something? You have this something? What is it?" Confused, Scarlett wonders if Amalie is sane. As soon as the idea crosses her mind, a sense of consequence negates it. She speaks Truth. That knowledge both surprises and confounds her. Back to her instincts. The instincts that never let her down.

"We don't know. That's where the magic part comes from. Not that we think the something is magic, just something we techno-mages haven't been able to identify. It's not genetics, though it is inherited about twenty percent of the time. It can't be taught unless you have that something. That something that I have. And you have."

Scarlett drops her mug. As if she was prepared, Amalie waves. A sudden glow of blue static arcs over her hands in a circuit-like pattern and the cup hovers in midair on its side. The mocha floats below, sloshing in a partial sphere as if caught in an invisible bowl. She moves her arm and the mocha pours back into the mug. Amalie reaches out and places the mug on a coaster, the static arcs disappearing as quickly as they appeared.

Scarlett had been about to scoff at the woman, but the act of... magic... freezes the exclamation in her throat.

Amalie touches a finger to Scarlett's chin and raises her head to meet her gaze. "Yes, you."

"But—"

She moves the finger to cover Scarlett's lips. "Shh. You need time to absorb this. And you need a distraction to let your mind work."

"A distraction? No. I think I need to concentrate. To think about it." This can't be possible? Can it? But I just saw it. Saw magic.

Amalie cups a hand on Scarlett's cheek. Scarlett leans into the touch as the woman across from her speaks. "Yes. Please trust me. You are a creative. You will intuit the information better if you don't dwell on it. Allow your creative side the freedom to work without your analytical side keeping you focused on what you've been taught about the world."

Scarlett asks, "What are you?"

Amalie's lips curl in a knowing smile. "I'm an analytical. Unlike you, I need to think things out. But that's me, not you. Please trust me." She leans in and kisses Scarlett, a long, soft and sensual kiss. Not demanding. Not taking, but inviting.

Scarlett moans. Amalie's lips are exquisite. She warms under the kiss, and when Amalie's tongue caresses her lips she allows it entrance. They spend long minutes in sensuous play; Scarlett doesn't remember a time a kiss has felt so much like her partner is caressing her soul.

Amalie whispers in-between panting breaths, her lips brushing against Scarlett's. "I want you. I wanted you since I first saw a picture of you. And when I met you, it was all I could do not to jump you right there in the front of the shop, witnesses be damned. Can I take you to my room?"

She wanted me too? A sense of relief floods through Scarlett; the attraction is mutual, and they are no longer in the shop. She no longer needs to stay professionally detached. "Yes."

***

They stumble up the narrow stairs; their hands wandering over each other. Scarlet manages to untie Amalie's robe at the same time the other woman yanks the tank over her head. Scarlett hops and pulls off her own shoes, dropping them to fall down a few steps. Seemingly impatient, Amalie leads her up the rest of the way and into the second door down the hall at the top.

"Lights, dim."

In the periphery of her awareness, Scarlett notices the light from downstairs goes out as the lamps in the room ignite in a comforting red glow. The bedroom is modest with a small amount of clutter and a queen-sized bed taking up most of the space.

Filling the room even more than the bed are the books. Every wall is covered in bookshelves from floor to ceiling, and every nook is crammed with paperbacks, hardbacks and leather-bound volumes.

The only interruption to the shelving is a small desk with a computer and large flat-screen monitor. Looking round, Scarlett sees more paperbacks stacked in a corner, and the nightstand looks like it will fall under the weight of more novels.

Amalie drops her robe, distracting Scarlett from her perusal of the room. The long smooth skin of her back is adorned with more of the circuit-like tattoos in black, in the shape of wings. A red circle with an intricate pattern on her tail-bone inspires feelings of energy and a rooting to reality. A dense tracery of green circuits trails from the red ink up her spine, before disappearing under her slightly longer than shoulder-length hair.

Scarlett wants to lick Amalie's spine, the art showcasing the grace and beauty of the other woman. With a jolt, she realizes she can and steps forward to touch the trail where the tattoo begins.

Amalie turns and takes her hands. "Give me a minute. I need to do one more thing before we start." She releases her hands and sits lotus style on the bed. The position exposes her shaved sex and Scarlett imagines running her mouth over it, her tongue between the folds.

She's snapped out of her reverie by Amalie's voice. Her face and neck heats under the caught-you-looking smile of the redhead.

Amalie waves a hand at her. "Strip."

Scarlett obeys the command, revealing her own ink along with her piercings. She matches the stereotype of a tattoo artist with her plethora of tattoos of varying sizes, shapes, styles, and colors. Portraits, flowers, birds, words, and geometric shapes are scattered in an almost haphazard array around her body. Some are simple and crude while others are masterpieces.

She has a double bar piercing in her left nipple and a belly button ring. When she finally drops her pants and panties, her totally bare mons is adorned by a simple silver ring in the hood of her clit.

Amalie places one hand on her lower back and the other on her own yellow circle. All of her chakra tattoos glow with the light of their color and the mysterious tattoos Scarlett thought she glimpsed earlier blossom with radiance. A blue circle adorns Amalie's throat, inspiring the urge to communicate with Amalie. An indigo pattern ignites on the woman's forehead, sharpening her vision and helping sort the thoughts of magic being real in her brain. And finally, though she can't see the design, violet shines through Amalie's glorious red tresses and pulls on her creative urges, almost dragging her from the moment to sketch.

A white glow shimmers across Amalie's form and when it fades, she emanates a sense of life and vitality that steals Scarlett's breath. She approaches the vision before her. As soon as she's near, Amalie reaches out and pulls her into a hungry demanding kiss. No more gentle teasing. Their connection is filled with want and lust, fueled by their desire for each other.

Scarlett crawls onto the bed, pushing Amalie down. Their breasts crush together in their embrace and an aching bolt of desire races from her chest. Amalie squirms and untangles her legs from underneath them to press a thigh into Scarlett's center while wrapping the other around her to pull her closer.

Unable to hold back any longer, Scarlet cries out and grinds herself onto the offered leg. The need painful, the pleasure glorious. She throws her head back and pumps her for a minute. The woman under her is like home and sin mixed in one sensuous package. She grunts out her orgasm as Amalie bites her pierced nipple.

After the quick release she falls against the woman, panting. Amalie runs her hands up and down the length of her back, letting her come down from her high. "Oh God I needed that. The sight of you writhing on my table just about drove me insane." The distraction, foretold by Amalie, had worked and a thought clicks into place in Scarlett's mind. "The ink! What's in the ink?"

Amalie curves her lips in a smile of a satisfied teacher and strokes Scarlett's face. "Nano-machines. They're suspended in all of the ink I have. They're what allow techno-mages to do their magic."

"Wait. I thought nano-machines were still too simple to be useful except as a curiosity." Scarlett's brow creases.

Amalie rubs her fingers over Scarlett's forehead, smoothing the frown. "We techno-mages are a bit... ahead of the curve. Plus, that special something is required to be able to control them and make them more than toys." She claims Scarlett's mouth in a thought-destroying kiss.

Scarlett's whole body warms, and arousal flows through her. Still too sensitive for more, she breaks from the kiss and works her lips across Amalie's throat. She only spends a moment on the flesh, just long enough to raise the warmth and heartbeat of the woman below her. She works down to her breasts, taking another look to confirm the tattoo is truly healed. The ink is vibrant. Whatever magic Amalie did healed the tattoo the instant it was created.

Satisfied, she licks across Amalie's breast, following the snake's body with little nibbles until arriving at the other breast. She claims the nipple being threatened by glistening fangs, and sucks fervently on the bud while sensuous moans escape the redhead. The feel of Amalie's body writhing under her is even more erotic than the memory of her on her table.

When Amalie grinds her center into Scarlett's belly, Scarlett follows the snake in the other direction, licking, nibbling, and biting the skin it covers until she reaches its tail.

The heady scent of female arousal that so teased her in her tattoo room forces her to inhale deeply and savor the smell. She gently rubs her nose on the small patch of red hair at Amalie's apex then licks from the bottom of her dripping wet folds. The salty-earthy taste of her lover gathers as her tongue licks over the hard nub of nerves. At the lightest touch on her clit, Amalie's hips buck.

Scarlett spends a few minutes running her tongue the length of the woman's core, flicking her tongue on her clit at the end of each trip. Amalie's writhing becomes more pronounced and the mewling sounds coming from her drive Scarlett on. She revels in the sensory overload of sound, scent, and touch. Finally she slides a finger into Amalie's sopping wet sex and swirls her tongue in a constant circle around her clit.

Intuition strikes, and when the clenching around her finger indicates Amalie is about to fly over the edge, Scarlett pulls back and blows on the small bundle of nerves. She waits until the orgasm is no longer imminent, then returns to her new favorite pastime of licking Amalie's clit.

She continues to bring Amalie to the brink and back off until the redhead is begging for release and her hands are tangled deep in Scarlett's black hair. With a flourish of her tongue, she ends the pleasurable torment and licks until Amalie stiffens then screams her name. Scarlet revels in the sensation of Amalie's center clenching her finger. She leaves it where it is as she moves up her lover's body giving her the comfort of lying on top of her while she rides out the aftershocks of her orgasm.

She's resting comfortably, enjoying the feel of the woman under her when Amalie chants some numbers. A flash of light dazzles Scarlett and suddenly, Amalie pushes her onto her back. Scarlett is stunned by the blazing lust she sees in the redhead's eyes and amazed at the amount of the energy the woman has after such a mind blowing orgasm. Right, the light. She charged herself again!

Amalie doesn't pause and nibbles over Scarlett's breasts, lavishing them with attention. As soon as Scarlett's arousal has her panting, Amalie slides a finger into her needy center. She pulls out to thrust in with a second, giving Scarlett exactly what she needs. She pauses from devouring Scarlett's breast and asks "How did you know I like edging?"

Scarlett shrugs "I just knew."

A huge beaming smile blooms on Amalie's face. "You're going to be so amazing when I teach you, if you'll let me. Can I show you the magic you helped me make today?"

Scarlett's barely able to think with Amalie's amazing fingers stroking slowly in and out. Each time she reaches full depth, her palm rubs against her clit and the ring in the hood, creating tingles of pleasure. She finally nods and lets out a breathy "Yes."

Amalie chants formulae for a minute, never stopping the rhythm of her fingers and palm. The chakra tattoos glow, their light intensifying as the mantra continues. With a final flare of brilliance, the snake comes alive and lifts from the techno-mage's breasts. With her free hand she strokes its head, and it seems to rub into the touch as if enjoying the contact.

Scarlett should be stunned or terrified. But instead everything comes together in her mind. The special ink, the glimpses of tattoos that weren't visible, the circuit patterns on Amalie's skin. The snake moving when the tattoo was complete. She smiles happy she wasn't imagining things and grateful the world is an even more amazing place than she already thought. "It's beautiful. We both do great work."

Amalie smiles. "Stay the night?"

Scarlett's chest fills with warmth. The urge to know the woman straddling her thigh, thrusting into her, and petting a living tattoo she created compels her to answer. "Yes. I'd like more. To get to know you more."

The smile of satisfaction on Amalie's face grows. She nods and leans down to lightly bite Scarlett's pierced nipple. "Then I have one more thing for you to experience."

Scarlett almost jumps when the snake wraps its body around her breast, moaning at the intense pressure when it squeezes. Amalie continues to lavish attention on her pierced nipple and moves her fingers into her core. The snake constricts and rubs her breast and flicks its tongue in a tickling caress on her other nipple. Scarlett watches as her gorgeous lover and the beautiful blue and red snake drive her higher and higher. When she's on the edge, Amalie pulls hard on her nipple at the same instance the snake strikes, its fangs piercing her other nipple. Heat and pleasure-pain flow with the venom into her right breast and she flies over the edge in the most consuming orgasm she has experienced.

Amalie strokes her cheek, whispering in her ear. "This is the start of something amazing."

ABOUT
THE AUTHORS

Lilya Loring

Lilya Loring has an unhealthy obsession with fairy tales. She received a Master of Fine Arts in Creative Writing in 2014. She lives in the South, surrounded by an ever-growing pile of books.

Zak Jane Keir

Zak Jane Keir has a long history of writing about sex. Though she mainly focuses on fiction now, she has written for magazines such as Forum and Penthouse in the past. She prefers writing contemporary femdom fiction and also runs the Dirty Sexy Words erotica slams.

Harley Easton

Harley Easton is a Renaissance woman dabbling in everything life offers. She's worked at a major theme park, found expert witnesses for legal cases, been a guest lecturer at a well-known national museum, and worked with medical students. Putting experience and insanity to good use, she's become an author specializing in erotic, romantic, and speculative fiction.

Gregory L. Norris

Gregory L. Norris grew up on a healthy diet of creature double features and classic SF TV shows. He once worked as a screenwriter on two episodes of Paramount's modern classic, Star Trek: Voyager, and is a former writer at SCI FI, the official magazine of the Sci Fi Channel (before all those ridiculous Ys invaded). Norris's short stories appear regularly in fiction anthologies, and he has published several collections and novels, two of the latter appearing on Home Shopping Network's "Escape with Romance" line, the first time HSN has made novels available to their customers.

Katya Harris

Katya Harris live in the UK with her boyfriend, kid, and the smuggest ex-stray cat in the world. She loves writing stories of lust and romance, and adores happy endings. She hopes you like what she's written and that you'll come back for more.

Victoria Blisse

Victoria Blisse is a mother, wife, Christian, Manchester United fan and award winning erotica author. She is also the editor of several Bigger Briefs collections, and the co-editor of the fabulous Smut Alfresco, Smut in the City and Smut by the Sea Anthologies.

Victoria is also one of the brains behind the fabulous

Smut events, days and nights dedicated to erotica, fun and prizes.

She is equally at home behind a laptop or a cooker and she loves to create stories, poems, cakes and biscuits that make people happy. She was born near Manchester, England and her northern English quirkiness shows through in all of her stories.

Passion, love and laughter fill her works, just as they fill her busy life.

Alain Bell

Alain Bell is a writer of lesbian erotic romances. Ze began as a game designer, a career that led to an enthusiasm for writing. Ze is passionate about LGBT rights and believes that love is love, romance is romance, and sex is erotic in whatever form it takes.

Anna Sky

This is Anna's first venture into editing and she's loved every second! As an erotica writer, she's been published by multiple presses and has self-published several of her own anthologies, one of which has even been quoted in a PhD thesis for short-story form! Apart from that she's (in no particular order) a geek, red wine drinker, poi hurler, Firefly fan, has a very dirty laugh and loves to perform research for her stories!

**And if you loved this anthology,
please leave a review!**

ABOUT
SINCYR PUBLISHING

At SinCyr Publishing, we wish to provide relatable characters facing real problems to our readers, in the sexiest or most romantic manner possible. Our intent is to offer a large selection of books to readers that cover topics ranging from sexual healing to sexual empowerment, to body positivity, gender equality, and more.

Too many of us experience body shaming, sexual shaming, and/or sexual abuse in our lives and we want to publish stories that allow people to connect to the characters and find healing. This means showing healthy BDSM practices, characters that understand consent and proper communication, characters that stare down toxic culture and refuse to take part... No matter what the content is, our focus is on empowering our readers through our books.